Emiss

Stories and Reflections by Dean William Rudoy

Emissaries

Stories and Reflections by Dean William Rudoy

Emissaries: Stories and Reflections by Dean William Rudoy

This edition has been published in 2022 in the United Kingdom by Paper + Ink.

www.paperand.ink
Twitter: @paper_andink
Instagram: paper_and.ink

The author wishes to acknowledge *The Intelligent Collector* magazine, with gratitude, for granting permission to use portions of his original essay "Recollecting the Kennedys" (Summer/Fall 2013) in the story "The Brothers," contained in this volume.

1 2 3 4 5 6 7 8 9 10

ISBN 9781911475590

A CIP catalogue record for this book is available from the British Library.

Jacket design by James Nunn: www.jamesnunn.co.uk | @Gnunkse

Printed and bound in Great Britain.

For all the children on the tree I planted, with this advice:

Now and then, step off the world and onto the Earth,
for there reside the answers to all our questions.

Oh, and always keep a window open in the attic.

Yes, I feel the moment has come for me to look back, if I can, and take my bearings, if I am to go on. If only I knew what I have been saying. Bah, no need to worry, it can only have been one thing, the same as ever. I have my faults, but changing my tune is not one of them. I have only to go on, as if there was something to be done, something begun, somewhere to go. It all boils down to a question of words, I must not forget this, I have not forgotten it. But I must have said this before, since I say it now.

Samuel Beckett, *The Unnamable*

Words, words, words!!
I'm so sick of words.
I get words all day through,
first from him, now from you.
Is that all you blighters can do?
Show me!

Eliza Doolittle

Author's Note

Where prudent, to respect the privacy of certain people mentioned in these pages, names have been changed and identifying characteristics altered. And so, while some of the stories may not be entirely real, they are all true.

Contents

Acknowledgments 11
Introduction: Watching the Wake 13

SHAPED AND BURNISHED 14
There's a Boy Growing in the Garden 15
You Know Things! 18
Would You Like a Cup of Coffee? 21
Birthmarked 25
Kindness to a Boy 28
Riding No-hands 30
Radish Seeds and Valentines 31
Shoes Polished / Streamers Flying 34
The Library 35
The Bench of Humiliation 36
I See You at the Top 39
The Slap of the Baton 41
We Could See Our Breath 43
Some Things Grow in the Dark 48
CO 51
The Copper Bracelet 54

MY PEOPLE 56
Mr Lucky 57
Something More to Learn / Something More to Teach 59
No Fear. No Regrets. 61
Bound to Obey 62
Looking for Signs 65
Into Debt to Give 67
Michail 69
The Atonement Tree 73
Daniel, My Friend for Life 76

IN MY CARE 78
Tommy 79
Bellevue 83
His Smile Comes Back to Me 89
The Door 91
The White Painting 96
Bending the Rules 98
To Memorize You 101
As If It Were Yesterday 103
I'm Not Sad 107
Farewell, My Patients 109

BIG SKY / LONG HORIZON 112
Collecting Some Dirt 113
It's in Here 115
Sacred Words Were Spoken 118
The Child in the Hill 120
The Arc 124
The Ambassadors 128
With Their Hands 131

EXTENDING THE PERIMETER 135
The Tree I Planted 136
Sale Canceled 141
Bella Italia 144
Returning 148
Annika in the Snow 150
Damned at the Wedding 152
Pain's Antidote 155
Touching 157

AS LUCK WOULD HAVE IT 160
Shylock's Star 161
It Could Have Been No Other Way 164
Surrender 169

Out of Print and Impossible to Find 173
Used 175
John Wanted You to Have This 177
The Brothers 179
Losing My Grip 185

Epilogue: Return to Eden 189

Acknowledgments

To all the precious leaves on the tree I planted—my brothers and sisters, nephews and nieces, all kin by choice, those that still cling to the branches and those that have entrusted themselves to the autumn breeze—all of whom have so generously provided wind for my sails and ballast for my hold on this voyage of a lifetime: thank you.

To my hometown, Oshkosh, where, one summer night, we gathered quietly on the lawn to watch the fireworks over the lake. It grew dark. Suddenly and explosively, the sky filled with bursting colors. By some error, they had all gone off at once. The display far exceeded all expectations, then vanished into thin air.

To every child I have ever met, each of whom has whispered to me this curious and wise instruction from the present moment in which they reside: *Remember the future. Anticipate the past.*

To Steve Ross, my dear friend for half a century, whose ardent love of words, both sung and spoken, has challenged and elevated my vocabulary and who, one day after patiently listening to my meandering monologue on the demands of a spiritual life, smiled at me and said: "It's easier to bow than to be."

To my ambassador from the reading world, my discerning editor, Mitchell Albert, who—like a trusted steward committed to the refinement of his gentleman before presenting him to the world—provided his insightful counsel throughout this endeavor: my salute. Way beyond polishing my prose, he offered a quality that has eluded me all these years: restraint. (And to Duncan Knowles, for passing along that one story to Mitch, which set everything in motion.)

And to you, my readers. Over the years, I have been told that I have a way with words—or was that, *"you sure have a lot of words."* In any case, I thought I'd have a go at it and write this book. Thank you for reading it.

*

"Against the weight of the world's sorrows it is the joint venture entered into by writer and reader—the writer's labor turned to the wheel of the reader's imagination—that produces the freedom of mind from which we gather our common stores of energy and hope."

Lewis H. Lapham, Editor, Lapham's Quarterly

Introduction: Watching the Wake

All my life, I've been nostalgic, even as a child. Always drawn to the stern of the boat, I look back to watch the wake, sometimes convincing myself that *this* is what determines my direction. Perhaps in some ways it does. The stories in this book are vivid recollections of past moments that have moved me forward.

Yet every memory and anticipation I have exist in only one place—the *present*—just as every experience of which I have written has delivered me to the narrow threshold of *here and now*, between the boundless realms of past and future.

Each also confirmed my kinship with every other being in this life, my inseparable connection to everyone and everything across both space and time, dimensions that seem to separate all phenomena but actually join them together. It's a matter of perception, really, but might require the slight tilting of one's head to see.

Within this book are stories of certainty and doubt, of the coincidence of opposites, of the appearance of helpful emissaries and healing epiphanies—and of an abiding hope in the promise of this hard, sweet life.

Come join me at the back of the boat …

SHAPED AND BURNISHED

"You don't look back. You keep your eyes ahead. And then, you run."

There's a Boy Growing in the Garden

Scripture tells us that God first planted a garden. Perhaps He knew what a comfort it would be. It's not a bad idea, occasionally, to pause to touch the earth from which we come—to recognize, as did Henry David Thoreau, that "Heaven is under our feet, as well as over our heads." A garden is a place to bear witness to the slower rhythms and cycles of Nature, the turning of the seasons, change and transformation, resilience and renewal: the arising, manifesting and dissolving of forms and patterns of the natural world, out of which we come, of which we are a part, and into which we disappear.

Plants invite us to be more human—to come down to earth. The very words *human*, *humility*, and even *humor* all have as their root the Latin word *humus*, meaning "earth." Because we are portable and plants are more or less stationary, and we name them and they do not name us, we sometimes lose sight of our kinship with them. But children know better.

Some time ago, I visited friends who have a son, then four years old. He had a big, red, rubber ball that he was tossing around the living room. One of his throws went astray and the ball hit a large, potted plant in the corner of the room. He ran to retrieve the ball, but on the way stopped to kiss the leaves of the plant.

Some of my fellow psychologists might say this is an example of projection or mistaken identification. I think it is an incidence of *recognition*. The boy recognized some similarity between himself and the plant. He knows he has feelings, and so the plant must have feelings as well. And he felt a responsibility to make amends.

What we see in this incident is not a child's mistake. What we see is the birth of morality.

The boy has *floodlight attention*; he sees the big picture. In time, he will learn *spotlight attention*. He will learn to name the parts of the plant, and how to distinguish and discriminate it from other plants. And, having learned all of these important distinctions, he will be no closer to the truth of what he knows now.

He knows now what sages and mystics seek for years to discover: the force that animates all life, the healing, restorative energy behind all forms, patterns, and masks. His intuitive knowledge may get buried beneath academic lessons, but it will resonate when he is in a garden.

And when the boy sits in a garden, he will notice important things that will console him later, when he feels the rough edges of this sometimes-difficult life. He will notice that wherever there is sunlight, there must necessarily be shadow, but that it is equally true that wherever there are shadows, there is bound to be light.

In the Jewish tradition, the groove above the upper lip is the impression left by an angel's finger: just before we are born, we know *everything*, and then an angel comes along and says, "*Shhhhh*" and touches us just there. And we come into this world innocent and ignorant—but not entirely. What child needs to be taught that a rainbow is beautiful? They *know* it, because within them is another held in memory.

In a sense, when a child is born, the universe is re-created. For at that moment, from a point in time and space that has never been occupied before, the universe is seen *for the first time*. Every child brings into this life a new perspective, and an ancient wisdom.

Perhaps because they look at the world from the ground up, children have an intuitive understanding that everything is alive and related; and they invite us to remember what we once knew.

There are times in our adult lives when we catch glimpses of the underlying energy and eternal presence behind the multitude of forms that we find in this world: birds and trees, rivers and wind, clouds and stones, four-year-old boys and large, potted plants. Such glimpses often appear just around the corner: in a garden, in the woods, in an open field, in the expansive, consoling desert.

When spring arrives, we should get out into the dirt. Feel it. Smell it. Dig our fingers into it. Plant something. And when those sprouts and buds make their miraculous and optimistic appearance, we should pause to consider this remarkable power of life, unfolding and unfolding, arising out of the dirt and reaching for the sun without looking back.

Children, as astonishing and hopeful as those plants, have a bold vision of a world that is free; a world without boundaries, without fears, without malice. They are emissaries of that truth. Their appearance amongst us is evidence of both a promise and a possibility.

Their vision is our hope.

You Know Things!

When I moved from New York City to the village of Corrales in New Mexico at the age of forty, I arrived with the intention of becoming a part of a small community and making some sort of contribution.

When I was a boy, the public library in Oshkosh, Wisconsin was a place of refuge and mystery. I loved books, and was an avid reader. Much of my life was spent inside my imagination—and still is. So I found my way to the village library, built by hand by the residents years before.

"Hello, my name is Dean Rudoy, and I just moved here. I'd like to volunteer."

"Great. Do you have any particular interests?"

"Well, if you have a children's program, I'd like to contribute something to that."

"We have Story Time every Wednesday morning at ten o'clock, but we already have a story reader."

"Maybe I could be a backup, whenever that person is not able to come in."

"That sounds good."

The following Wednesday, I arrived for Story Time, just to get the lay of the land. Sitting in a straight-backed chair was an elderly woman reading in a rather heavy German accent to a half-dozen preschool kids. The book had no pictures. She turned a page and screamed, thrusting the book toward the children: "You see this! This is called a 'dog-ear.' Someone borrowed this book and bent this page. This is a *terrible* thing to do, and very selfish!" The kids looked scared.

A week later, I was called to fill in. I arrived with four books in hand. One of them was titled *Caps for Sale*, and was about a man who traveled from village to village with all the hats he was selling stacked on top of his head. He fell asleep under a tree; the monkeys who lived in the branches grabbed his hats, and the fun began. I brought a bunch of different hats with me: fedora, beret, cowboy hat, baseball cap, and a few others. After the story, the children and I had a good time trying on the hats and talking about why they looked like they did, and what they were for.

I set aside the chair and remained on my knees during the hour in order to be at the same height as the kids, who sat in front of me. We read the books together, counted and named colors and shapes, and talked about dogs and cookies and spiders.

I was invited back the following week—and the week after that, and the next. I don't know what happened to the Story Time lady, but now that hour, every Wednesday morning, was called "Story Time with Dr Dean." And that's the way it was for the next ten years of reading stories and discussing life with preschool kids.

During that time, I learned to always start with the most complex of the four books and end with a book that was just about colors and shapes—which respected the attention spans of the kids. I also learned that I could occasionally lob a comment over the heads of the children sitting on the carpet to the parents sitting on chairs behind them. These were usually ironic, and the grown-ups seemed to like them.

I also learned that books awaken ideas in kids. Once, when I was reading about a boy and his dog, one youngster urgently exclaimed: "My dog died."

Down went the book. "What was your dog's name?"

"Barnaby."

"Will you tell us a story about Barnaby?" He did.

Then a little girl had a story about her cat—and other kids followed. After a few minutes, we all fell silent.

"Shall we return to the book?" Nods—and so we did.

I also learned that I didn't need to set any rules. As the number of kids grew—often up to forty, and once fifty—the chattering inspired by the stories occasionally got out of hand. "I can't hear any *one* of you when *all* of you are talking. What can we do about that?"

After a few moments, one of the kids said: "Maybe we can raise our hands."

"Sounds good. Let's try that." And so, a social rule was born out of our society.

Once, while showing them a picture of some balloons and flowers and stars in book no. 4, I said: "Now, look at this picture and remember everything you see." They stared. I closed the book. "How many balloons did you see?"

"We don't know. We didn't count them."

"Close your eyes and remember." They all closed their eyes. In a moment, a hand went up: "Four balloons."

I opened the book and we looked. "Four balloons! You see, you *know things*."

And so a tradition was born.

I was at the village post office picking up mail one day, when I ran into one of the moms of the Story Time kids. "Dr Dean, I want you to know that my boy has a hard time getting out of bed, *except* on Wednesdays. On those mornings, he yells out: 'Let's go see Dr Dean! He says we *know* things.'"

After ten years of Wednesday mornings, I moved away from Corrales. The library threw a going-away party for me.

"You can't leave yet," said a pregnant mom, touching her belly. "You have to stay to read to my son."

"Oh, but I've been reading to him all along."

And a father approached me. "I want you to know something before you go. You taught me to respect my children." Although that had not been my intention, this dad had watched and learned.

The gal who was going to take over Story Time took me aside: "I can't replace you."

"Nope, none of us can replace any of us, but you will succeed me."

"Can you give me any advice?"

I did: "Just remember, Story Time is not about the books."

Would You Like a Cup of Coffee?

What fun it was to visit Grandma Becky's house in Manitowoc, Wisconsin—the house in which my mom grew up. It *smelled* different: fragrances of thousands of home-cooked meals. And it had a staircase! Having been raised in a split-level home, I knew nothing of steps, but welcomed the experience of climbing up and down—which I did often, even though I wasn't going anywhere in particular. It was the friendly creaking I enjoyed most.

We were to spend the night on one such visit, and I was filled with excited anticipation of sleeping in a different bed and awakening in a different home. Grandma had a huge linen closet and was well-prepared for us. Back in earlier years, it was not uncommon to have family visit for long stretches of time.

That first morning, awakened by the exhilarating smell of coffee, I padded down the stairs, making sure to bounce on the step that made the most noise, into the kitchen, where my mom and her mom sat talking. The percolator was on the stove, popping insistently.

"Would you like a cup of coffee?"

I looked behind me, to see who Grandma was talking to. There was no one.

She looked at me. "Well?"

I looked at my mom. She nodded.

"Yes, please."

I could hardly contain myself as my mom reached into the china cabinet to select a cup and saucer—the very ones she had been responsible for collecting when she was a girl, and movie houses gave away Fiesta chinaware to patrons. Suddenly before me was a yellow cup and saucer. Grandma poured in a bit of coffee and then topped it off with lots more milk. Oh, and plenty of sugar.

I blew on the top of the liquid, just like a grown-up, and then sipped. Quite honestly, I had never tasted anything so delicious before—or since.

My Uncle Melvin would always join us. He was a storyteller. He'd just make them up, about himself and his friend Pete, when they were boys. Or maybe they were true. I never knew; but they were enchanting adventures about simple things like going for a hike, or a bike ride, or a trip to the zoo. Uncle Melvin was the first of only a few people in my life who accepted me just as I was. My Aunt Mary gave me that same embrace throughout my life. Those are rare gifts for a child to receive, the memory of which has seen me through many difficult times.

*

When we drove to Green Bay to visit Grandpa Harry and Grandma Bessie, my dad's folks, we would always stop at a diner midway, where I would have my favorite of all meals, an open-faced hot turkey sandwich: white bread, slices of turkey, mashed potatoes, cranberry sauce, and, of course, lots of gravy. The food was so soft, you hardly had to chew.

As we approached my grandparents' neighborhood, I knew just when to lean out the window to look for the sign.

"There it is, Grandpa and Grandma's house!"

The sign was mounted beside the front door of the modest house and it simply said, MIRRORS RESILVERED. It was shiny and reflected the light. Grandpa was a mirror maker.

Grandpa and Grandma would always welcome us outside, and then we'd climb the steps and enter the living room, where we would sit on the plastic-covered sofa. In fact, everything was covered in plastic, including the lampshades. It wasn't until many years later that I understood that, given their experience of extreme poverty, the main intent in owning anything was not *comfort*; it was *preservation*. But back then, all I knew was that that sofa was awfully cold to the touch in winter, and awfully sticky on the back of my legs in summer.

All the grown-ups spoke Yiddish, a language I felt I knew but didn't. My grandparents knew very little English. But one thing Grandpa did know how to say, he would always say after chasing me around in the backyard, grabbing me from behind, rubbing his rough cheek against mine and whispering into my ear:

"You know what?"

"What, Grandpa?"

"I love you."

They had raspberry bushes in that backyard, and Grandma would make something the likes of which I had never seen. She'd wash and drain the berries, put them into a plastic container mixed with an abundance of sugar, and freeze them. At some point in our visits, especially in the summertime, she would hand me one of these containers with a spoon and I'd dig in, not realizing that more than a half-century later it would be one of my favorite memories.

*

Many years later, as an adult, I went to visit my folks in Hollywood, Florida, where they lived in a handsome condominium at the edge of a golf course. One evening, we went to the country club for dinner. There we were with several of their friends, sitting at a big, round table. We had a good meal and, while we were having coffee and dessert, I asked if anyone spoke Yiddish, as I had not heard it in many years. Everyone denied knowing any.

Pause.

Then, someone said something in that old-world tongue, to which another protested: "That isn't how you say it!"

"Yes, it is!"

And then chaos ensued, as everyone started speaking Yiddish, loudly. I didn't understand a word of it, but it was wonderful.

You see, how one speaks Yiddish, which words they use and how they are pronounced, depends upon the *shtetl* in which your people lived before they made their way to America. Kvetching and arguing about these things is fundamental to speaking the language.

Another thing we argue about is how to spell the names of our holidays. For example, is it *Chanukah* or *Hanukkah*? Over many years, hours of loud and fruitless disagreements have been spent on this essential point, despite the fact that it doesn't matter. All English spellings of Hebrew or Yiddish words are transliterations of words in their original languages. But, oh, what fun to quarrel and shout!

When Grandpa Harry died, my dad asked if there was anything of his I would like to have.

"May I have the sign?"

And so my dad drove to Green Bay and pried the sign off Grandpa's house. Today it hangs on the wall at my front door. I touch it sometimes.

Birthmarked

Every family creates a bit of mythology to explain unforeseen circumstances. When I was born, I was very dark, a fact which, I regret to say, was something of an embarrassment to my family. Indeed, unlike most family albums proudly stocked with photos of the newly arrived, ours contained only a couple of pictures of me as a baby. A story was born that I was a changeling.

On top of that, I had two tiny birthmarks—one on the bottom of my right foot, in the middle of the sole, and one in the middle of my forehead. No story was made of these, but they have always intrigued me. Did something pass through me?

My very first memory is one of defiance. I was sitting in my highchair. My mom put some scrambled eggs on the tray. I grabbed them in my fists and threw them to the floor. Even I was startled by my appalling lack of manners.

At age two, I almost died from a severe case of pneumonia; the fever was so high, I was bathed in alcohol to bring it down.

As time went by, I lightened up just a bit, but summer always revealed my birthright: my body turned bronze, and my true color reappeared. The birthmarks became more distinct. And throughout childhood, I continued to suffer respiratory ailments.

I also had bad dreams. One night, I awoke from a nightmare in which a witch hovered over me on her broomstick. When she slowly reached down and touched me in the small of my back with her finger, I awoke with a start, threw off my covers, and jumped on top of my bed. I caught sight of my reflection in the mirror on the wall.

"Night mirror!" I said to myself (my juvenile understanding of the word *nightmare*), and climbed back under the covers, which I was convinced were impenetrable to anything that might harm me.

I was a moody child, prone to sad thoughts, although of course there were times of great happiness. I discovered early on that the very depth of joy is where sorrow will reach. My parents were aware of this tendency, and, employing an old Jewish custom, would occasionally blow on top of my head to dispel the dark brooding. Sometimes that worked, and anyway, it felt good. Sometimes it didn't.

In their discomfort and helplessness at witnessing their son suffer, they told me, "You have too many feelings."

Now, what is a child to do with that assessment from people upon whom he is utterly dependent? Well, he couldn't stop having feelings, but he could stop showing them. I remember the exact moment I decided never to cry again.

There are consequences to suppressing one's feelings. In addition to my chronic respiratory issues, I developed digestive problems and an unsightly repertoire of nervous facial tics. Clearly, something was going on inside.

Many years later, while pursuing doctoral studies in psychology, I decided that the best way to learn the practice of psychotherapy would be to watch it close up by being in therapy myself. Besides which, having by nature more of a shadow disposition than sunny, dark thoughts were still my occasional companion, and I had no one to blow on top of my head.

I began my search. I wanted a therapist who had been psychoanalytically trained, someone who would work with me in-depth. During that time, I had a remarkable dream. I was in the East, perhaps India, and walking outside in the sunlight beside the glass wall of a building. I caught sight of my reflection: I was young, with dark skin and very long black hair, and wore a loose, traditional shirt, a *kurta*. My feet left the ground, and I began to float into the air. There were children in the courtyard, playing with a large ball. Laughing, they threw it up to me. I caught it and tossed it back down, smiling at them.

Several weeks later, on the advice of a friend, I made an appointment with a therapist. Her name was Phyllis. She was from Sri Lanka, and spoke with the lovely, lilting accent of people from that place. Her skin was dark, and she wore a *sari*. I felt right at home.

Phyllis and I worked together for five and a half years. Of course, there are many stories, but I'll relate only one. It is emblematic of who she was to me.

One day, she told me that in the event I arrived early, I should look down the hall from the waiting room; if her door was open, I would be welcome to enter. Now, you need to understand what an extraordinary invitation that was. Every minute of therapy is precious; the prospect of more time than allotted was exhilarating.

Well, one day I arrived for my appointment a bit early. I peeked tentatively around the corner down the hall. Her door was open, so I approached. When I entered the room, Phyllis was sitting in her big chair, reading *The New York Times*. The moment she caught sight of me, she lay the newspaper down. Smiling brightly, she opened her hands in welcome, gesturing for me to come in. She had set the world aside for me.

I sat down and cried unshed tears, blended together over all the years. I wasn't sure from which experience they came. Perhaps from boyhood, when I held my eyes tight so the tears would not flow, and I would be a man. You see, when I was little, and my father would come home from work and sit in his big chair with the newspaper in front of him, I might approach with a drawing I had made that I wanted to show him.

"Daddy … Daddy? Daddy?" The newspaper remained in place.

At the end of my final session with Phyllis, after years of working together, we rose from our chairs and stood silently in front of one another.

She took my face in her hands and said: "In the great confluence of the universe, how fortunate that we met."

Kindness to a Boy

Back in the 1950s, we had milk delivered to the house. Mr Janke would make his rounds early in the morning, collecting empties and refilling the little metal box we had out at the back door. On hot summer days, we kids would chase his truck down Oak Street.

"Mr Janke! Mr Janke! Give us some ice, please."

Mr Janke would stop his truck and get out, smile at us, and walk to the back, open the big door, chip off generous chunks of crystal-clear ice with his pick, and hand them around.

"Thanks, Mr Janke!"

And off he'd drive.

We'd stand there in the middle of the street under the searing sun, ice-cold water dripping through our fingers, carefully holding our precious pieces as if they were diamonds. And we'd lick them.

*

Harry was a policeman. He was a big, tall, red-haired guy who, on his off-hours, took care of our lawn until I was old enough to take that on as part of my chores. I used to follow him around as he cut the grass and raked up the debris. He was awfully nice to me, and never gave me the sense that I was bothering him.

It was around that time that I pretended that I was an undercover cop. Whenever I'd be out riding my bike and see a police car, I'd nod, and they'd nod back—in recognition, I was sure, of my special standing with the force.

One afternoon, when the county fair was in town, some pals and I walked over to the fairgrounds, our allowances jingling in our pockets in hopes of winning something big. Harry was in uniform, directing traffic. When he saw me, he held out his arms and stopped all the cars, nodding to my friends and me that we could cross safely. I was a hero from that day on to my pals, and Harry was a hero to me.

*

When I started collecting stamps as a kid, I used to get these enormous bags of used stamps from all over the world for just a buck or two. During that time I was introduced to King George VI. *Who is this guy on all these stamps from so many countries?* I pulled out the *World Book Encyclopedia* and studied up on him, and on the British Empire. Later, when I learned more about his personal story of reluctantly assuming the throne upon the abdication of his brother, of his devotion to duty, of his valor during World War II, of his arduous work to overcome his disabling stammer, he became one of the men in my life to whom I looked for inspiration.

As time went by, I narrowed my collecting interests to just US stamps. I was particularly captivated by what are called plate blocks—the four stamps in the corner of a sheet that also contained the printing plate number in the margin. When I read of a new stamp in one of my stamp-collecting newsletters, I'd bike over to the post office to see if it had come in. The postmaster would greet me at the counter: "Hello, Dean, we just got in a new stamp, and I saved the block for you."

"Wow! Thanks a lot!"

He'd hand it to me in a little glassine envelope to protect it, and I'd hand over the sixteen cents.

He'd thought about me even before I was there in front of him. That always surprised me.

*

One day, a fire truck went speeding by, lights flashing, sirens screaming. I ran outside to see one of the firemen's hats fly off his head and roll down the street. I ran fast to retrieve it. The truck stopped. Breathlessly, I handed the hat up to the man.

"Thanks, pal."

And off they sped.

Thanks, pal. That has stayed with me all my life, as have all of the simple kindnesses during those early years shown by those already grown to a small boy.

Riding No-hands

It's springtime in the desert. The golden grasses are already knee-high, the sage is bushy with new smoky-green growth, and the cactus blooms with bright yellow flowers. I'm sitting at an outdoor café in a small New Mexico village. Having carefully placed my cup of coffee, glass of water, and slice of fresh-baked apple cake next to my tablet and pencil on a wobbly, wrought-iron table, I wait for an idea to write about.

I arrived here by bicycle, during which I rode "no-hands" for a distance, balancing while rolling up my sleeves on this hot May afternoon. Sixty years ago, the feat of riding no-hands—let alone on two wheels—was something of a dream for me. My main goal in life at that time was to ride my blue and white Schwinn *without* training wheels down the sidewalk under the huge, arching trees that lined Oak Street.

I remember being determined every day not to fall *this time.* I'd climb on, balance with my toes, and push off. But that front wheel had a life of its own. I'd zig and zag just a few feet before gravity would pull me down hard once again. Then, one evening, after a couple of hours of persistent but failed attempts, my mom called out that it was time to come in.

Well, I was about half a block away. *I can walk the bike home or try one more time,* I thought to myself. Clenching my jaw, I slung my right leg over the bike, mounted the seat, and touched the sidewalk with the toes of my Converse All-Stars. I pushed forward a bit, then backward, just to get the feel of it. A deep breath. I slowly pushed off. My feet found the pedals and pumped right, left, right, left. Leaning forward, hands tightly gripping the handlebars, the bike jiggled a bit at first, but then: steady as she goes. The warm evening air washed across my face. I braked just before hitting the garage door. I had done it!

As time went by, I decorated my bike with the sights and sounds of childhood: a loud silver bell to announce my approach, plastic streamers exploding out of the handlebar grips, and the ace of spades flapping in the spokes, held down by a purloined clothespin.

Radish Seeds and Valentines

As a kid, I spent most of my allowance at the five-and-dime, on stamps for my collection (which awakened a fascination with the world and its diversity of countries and cultures); crayons (burnt sienna being my favorite); construction paper (the many-colored pack, the texture and smell of which delighted me); plastic models (painting them sent me into reveries); and electronic kits (the construction of which magically extended my senses).

Most of those important purchases are now lost to memory. Two significant ones remain: radish seeds and valentines.

*

The very first thing I ever planted, right next to the low juniper bushes in front of the house, were radishes. I didn't tell anyone. Every day, a little water; suddenly, fresh green sprouts. It was hard being patient, but every day, kneeling before them, I would compare what was growing to the picture on the seed packet. *When it looks like this,* I told myself, *I can harvest them.* What a thrill to pull them up: dark green leafy stems, bright red fruits, covered with rich, black soil.

I presented them to my mom in the kitchen late one afternoon and said: "For dinner."

"Where in the world did you get these?"

"I planted them. They're mine."

We washed them carefully. And that evening, I fed my family.

*

In second grade, in anticipation of Valentine's Day, we all brought in shoeboxes to decorate. While my classmates cut fancy hearts out of construction paper and pasted them on, sometimes festooned with glitter, I simply wrapped aluminum foil around the cardboard. Pretty flashy, but I liked shiny things. We put our names on our boxes and cut a slit at the top, into which valentines would be inserted on the appointed day.

I hopped on my bike and made it over to Woolworth's on Main Street, my allowance in my pocket. Once inside, I walked quickly past all the stamps, crayons, construction paper, and model kits, lest I be tempted, and made my way to the greeting-card section.

I knew that I wanted to give everyone in class a valentine, so I picked a bag filled with small, two-sided cards. Okay, done. Now, the hard part: I wanted to give larger cards that actually opened up and came with envelopes to several special friends. I plucked cards one by one off the display and looked inside each of them to read the message. This took quite some time, but it was important. I made my choices and brought everything to the register.

"You must have a lot of friends."

"I guess so."

Blushing, I left the shop, jumped on my bike, and headed home. Upon arriving, I went to my room and wrote the names of my classmates on all of the smaller cards. I decided to write something special inside the larger cards.

One of those larger cards was for Frankie.

Back in those days, long before classrooms were segregated by ability and subsequently reunited by mainstreaming, everyone of a certain age was in class together. We had kids who were really good at reading and writing and arithmetic mixed up with kids who weren't. In retrospect, I've often thought about how that experience made me a better person. Being in the presence of those who were struggling in school gave me the opportunity, at a very young age, to help other people, and I discovered how good that felt.

Frankie was what we called, in those days, *retarded.* She was also poor. Sadly, even at the age of eight, children can be cruel, and Frankie was the subject of much teasing and ridicule. However, despite the callousness of the classroom, she was often happy. That always puzzled me—but I admired her for it.

On Valentine's Day, our teacher gave us the signal to go around the room distributing our cards into the boxes. As anticipated, very few people stopped by Frankie's box to leave a loving sentiment. When I got there, I carefully inserted the biggest card I had.

When I think back on those days, about the boy I was, about what he planted in the soil and in people's hearts, I think I would have loved him.

Shoes Polished / Streamers Flying

One of my chores was to polish my father's shoes. I think he considered it a rather onerous task. What he didn't know was that I loved doing it.

I would clean them, vigorously rub paste polish in with my fingers (which is really the only proper way to do it), brush them hard, and finish them off with the polishing cloth. *Snap.*

They shined.

I'd then place them carefully in a straight line at the front door for him to inspect upon returning home from work. Sometimes he'd pause to admire them; sometimes he'd just walk by. I'd get fifty cents for each pair. But my pride in my work far exceeded the monetary compensation or the occasional acknowledgment.

I remember the satisfaction of good work done by hand, and the gratification of knowing when I was finished—a rare experience for those of us so often stuck in the unceasing clamor of our minds.

My wealth in my pocket, I'd jump on my Schwinn bike and pedal as fast as I could up New York Avenue, streamers flying from the handlebars, playing card firmly gripped by clothespin and clicking in the spokes, up a dozen blocks to the train tracks where Walter's Food Towne welcomed patrons with a maze of short aisles and a single cash register.

I'd lay my bike down in front of the shop—no chain, no lock. No one would steal your bike: a simpler time. Into the shop and right up to the thrilling, multicolored displays of candy and gum. There, Milk Duds and Red Hots, licorice and candy dots, bubble gum and lemon drops. Reaching into my pocket, I'd find the coins, feeling each one—Washington quarters, Mercury dimes, Buffalo nickels, Lincoln pennies—ready to be traded in for sugar in all its marvelous variety.

Back outside, I collected my bike and headed home, pumping the pedals, chewing on a braid of licorice, red and sweet.

Walter's Food Towne is long gone, but the train tracks are there, as is Oshkosh—where the winter wind can take your breath away, and where the moon still shines on the frozen lake.

The Library

Come back with me to the summer of 1959. The place: Oshkosh, my backyard. I'm ten years old. It's a hot, sunny day. I've just mowed the lawn, and am taking a well-deserved rest in the old hammock. I reach for my book and lift it up between the sun and me. A slight breeze mixes the sweet fragrance of freshly cut grass with the somewhat musty smell of the soft manila pages. I settle in and begin to read about my pals Henry and his dog Ribsy—and soon I am no longer in my backyard, but theirs.

I met Henry and Ribsy—and many other friends throughout my childhood—at the Oshkosh Public Library, where I recall being treated by the librarian with a degree of respect uncommon in my childhood experience, and before whom I was required to give a brief oral report on each book I read when I returned it (my first experiences in public speaking). There I made many discoveries exploring the stacks, and was introduced to classical music. What joy to be able to borrow concertos, symphonies, operas. I pretended the whole collection was mine—and in a way it was, for that is what community libraries are: each citizen's personal treasure house.

It was at the Oshkosh Public Library that I was also introduced to high technology: the copy machine. What a wonder, even though it took about five minutes to make a copy, which came out as a wet, negative print that smelled sort of funny. Never mind; I now owned a page from the *Encyclopaedia Britannica*.

In December 1963, deeply wounded by the recent loss of my hero, President Kennedy, I asked the librarian if I might set up a memorial display in the large glass case in the front lobby. She said okay. Creating that display for everyone to see somehow helped me through that difficult time.

Over the years there have been many libraries in my life, but it is always that first, in my hometown, to which I return in my mind—a place where I could browse without being shooed away, where I could hold ideas in my hands, a place of imagination, discovery, and sometimes retreat … a place where, if you were not allowed to have a dog, Henry would share his with you.

The Bench of Humiliation

When I was about nine years old, my dad bought me a baseball mitt. Now, for most boys, this would be cause for celebration. For me? Terror.

"Let's go outside and play some catch."

I was scared because I didn't know how. Besides which, the glove was stiff, and too big for my hand.

We went out in the backyard after dinner. He tossed the ball to me. I aimed the mitt toward it, but it escaped my reach. I ran after it and threw it back, underhanded.

"Don't throw like a girl."

Those dreaded words—a piercing epithet I would hear throughout my childhood that, while meant to deride me in particular, succeeded also in degrading all of the female sex.

After a few minutes of failed attempts to make a baseball player of me, my dad went inside. I stood there alone on the grass, just beyond the perimeter of my father's heart, as evening turned to night.

He handed the responsibility over to Little League, which proved fruitless. I couldn't catch. I couldn't throw. And every time up at bat, I struck out. It was the same with anything involving a ball—football, basketball, tennis, golf. It wasn't that I didn't try. On the contrary, I tried so hard I missed every time. Ball sports require a flexible connection and a sort of nonchalance, difficult to experience when utterly preoccupied with trying to win one's father's approval.

Thankfully, I did excel in track and field: running, broad jumping, and high jumping. And I wasn't too bad at fencing. In riflery, I won an array of sharpshooting awards. In fact, I was so steady and accurate that, before competitions, I was given all the team's .22-caliber rifles to shoot in order to align their sights. But none of this fully compensated for not being able to throw overhanded from right field—which is where the weakest player is always placed, and where I prayed no fly ball would come my way.

Even more than baseball, water was my nemesis. I was afraid of it. As we lived on a lake, my folks were determined that I should learn to swim, so they enrolled me in classes at the Y. A total novice, I was classified as a "minnow" and placed in a class of six-year-olds. I was nine at the time, and at least a head taller than my classmates—hardly the most conducive setting in which to learn the art of the fishes. To this day, the smell of a chlorinated pool awakens feelings of dread.

I was sent to summer camp. Given all of the above, you can imagine that the experience was, at best, mixed. Trying to fit in and make friends, I did my best to avoid the sports in which I had no ability (although some activities were mandatory), and gravitated toward those in which I did. I also spent a lot of time in the crafts lodge and darkroom. Swimming, however, was required of all campers. Having lost patience with me, a counselor one day told me to get into a canoe with him and paddle. This didn't seem so bad, as I really liked canoeing, and was quite good at it.

"Where are we going?"

"To the middle of the lake." That sounded rather ominous. When we got there, he said: "Get out."

Get out? Was he kidding? He wasn't, and, as he was a counselor and I just a kid, I had little say in the matter. I slowly climbed over the edge, holding tight to the gunwale of the canoe.

"Let go of that."

I let go, panicked, and sank immediately, gasping for air. Eventually, he jumped in and 'saved' me. There are some things that adults do to children that are simply unforgiveable.

One thing toward which I seemed somewhat naturally inclined in childhood was music. I enjoyed playing piano, and had even composed a couple of tunes. Mostly, I just liked to play around.

I was sent for lessons. About a year into them, my teacher scheduled a recital at the home of one of her students. I prepared two pieces: one I had learned, and one I had composed, both memorized. The day arrived, and my mom took me. Plastic folding chairs had been set up in the living room. I was nervous. When my turn came, I got up and walked to the piano.

When I sat on the bench I noticed that instead of white and black keys, the keys were white and brown. Given my anxiety, that was enough to send everything spinning. I tried to play, but found I couldn't go on, after only a few measures. The room fell silent. I got up and returned to my mom, who had the sheet music. I took it, made the long walk back to the keyboard, sat down, set up the music, and tried to play; but the notes were swimming in front of me. I stood up and walked back to my chair. Turning to my mom, I whispered: "I'm never doing that again."

What had been fun in play had become frightening in performance. I quit lessons. Today I regret having done so, because now, when I sit down at the piano for my own enjoyment, I play rather like a ten-year-old.

What is to be made of all these lasting impressions stamped on the warm wax of my childhood? *Too much too soon. Too little too late.*

As all parents do, mine drew an outline of expectation around me. As all children do, I failed to fulfill that silhouette. Like every child, I brought into this life my own being, my own gifts, the contours of which I asked to be accepted as they were. Though we never spoke of this, my parents and I reached something of an agreement. In many ways, they nurtured my nature. And in those ways that they could not, I became sensitive to the needs of other children whose gifts remain unclaimed, and developed an empathic awareness that has served me well.

I See You at the Top

Back in seventh grade, we had a tumbling unit in gym class. You know the drill: somersaults, the pommel horse, rings, and rope. I wasn't too terrible at the first three, but the rope was my adversary. I'd get halfway up, lose heart, and have to come down.

There were three ropes suspended from the I-beam on the ceiling—about twenty feet up. We'd form three lines, march up to the rope, and climb. My classmates were like monkeys, scrambling up to the top, hitting the I-beam with the palms of their hands, and climbing back down. As easy as that.

One day, having tried the rope and failed yet again, I was walking with the other guys to the locker room. I guess I was looking pretty dejected, head down and shuffling my feet. Mr Potterton, our teacher, discreetly folded himself into the group as we proceeded to the showers. He put his hand on my shoulder and said, "It seems you're having some problems with the rope."

"Yeah."

"Well, all I can tell you is that I see you at the top."

I stopped walking and turned to look at him. He was serious. I split off from the group and went to the rope, my heart beating pretty fast.

I grabbed hold of it with my right hand, and hoisted myself up: left hand, right hand, left hand, right hand. When I reached the top, I hit the beam with the palm of my hand.

Many years later, I wrote to Mr Potterton to tell him that I was now a psychologist working with street kids in New York City, and to thank him for what he had done. I was now passing along his gift of encouragement to these kids, I added. He wrote back that he didn't remember the incident, but that he was glad he had said the right thing at the right time.

And that's the thing. He always did.

A couple of years later, in ninth grade, I played second-string fullback on the football team. Being seriously nearsighted and restricted from playing with my glasses on was quite a challenge, plus the fact that I was pretty small compared to the other guys.

Nonetheless, Coach Potterton would send me in occasionally to run the one play I could do, a fullback sweep.

One afternoon, he noticed my father at the game on the sidelines, with his camera. He made a point of calling me over to him. I got off the bench and ran to his side. He stood there with his hand on my shoulder giving me instructions—long enough for my dad to get the shot—before I ran out onto the field. I still have that photograph ... and that memory.

If Coach taught me anything, it's that sometimes a kid only needs a single word of encouragement from an adult they admire, "the right thing at the right time," to climb beyond their own expectations.

The Slap of the Baton

When I woke up, I pulled the drapes away from the windows, and all I saw was, well, nothing. A huge snowdrift overnight had completely covered that side of the house. Snow Day! But, no. In Oshkosh, there were plenty of snowplows to clear the streets. Snow days were rare.

After breakfast—Mom's 'stick-to-your-ribs' oatmeal—I put on my corduroys, shirt and sweater, heavy parka and boots, and made it out the door. The snow was pristine and bright, glistening in the sun. The high drifts invited. During the night, a frozen crust had formed about an inch thick all along their crests. The challenge was to walk on top of the drifts, carefully transferring my weight from foot to foot, one quiet step at a time, trying not to break through and plunge into the several feet of powder below (all the while secretly hoping I would). Of course, this had to be done backwards, as the wind coming off the lake would steal one's breath if facing into it. Upon arriving at school, everyone exchanged notes on their drift escapades. Clean or powder-covered, their coats told the whole story.

Lake Winnebago, just across the street from our house, would freeze over in the winter. After dinner, I'd grab my skates and walk over there. It would be dark already, but if the moon was out, you could still pretty much see where you were going. My cap, without which Mom insisted I not leave the house, was safely tucked into my coat pocket—where it would remain for the duration of my adventure. My uncovered ears would turn bright red out in the frigid night-time air (which they still do sixty years later, at the slightest hint of a freeze).

The problem with skating on a frozen lake is that it's not flat. There are ripples and ridges across the surface. One evening, I mistakenly grabbed my figure skates rather than my hockey skates. Oh, well: I sat on a rock, put them on and went out. Within a couple of minutes, the inevitable happened. The front teeth of one of the blades caught hold of a bump, and I slammed into the ice, right onto my knee. I hobbled home.

The pain and swelling were so severe we called a doctor, who came to the house and inspected my knee. X-rays the next day confirmed a small crack. However, given my age at the time, it was decided I should just rest and stay off the ice while the bone healed on its own. I walked with a cane for a while, which drew a good deal of attention, and everyone wanted to hear the story, which, to be honest, became embellished over time. To this day, I still sport an impressive bump on my knee, which arouses people's interest and summons the telling of the tale.

A couple of years later, my knee now healed, I was on the junior high school varsity track and field team. The fact that I was quite good at running dashes and relays, broad jumping, and high jumping compensated for the fact that I could not throw a ball; and the fact that I was the anchor man in the men's 440-yard relay made me something of a hero. Of the four men, the anchor man is the last and fastest runner on the team, to whom the baton is passed. It is he who crosses the finish line. When you are at the ready, muscles tensed, body leaning far forward on the balls of your feet, the crowd cheering, you extend your arm backward, awaiting the baton from the previous runner. You don't look back. You keep your eyes ahead. And then you run.

Being on the track and field team taught me a lot about both competition and camaraderie, about winning, losing, and feeling the collective embrace of a steadfast group of friends. But mostly, it taught me about trust. That certain slap of the baton into the palm of my hand always confirmed it.

We Could See Our Breath

We could see our breath in the cold night air as we tromped through the snow of the parking lot to the church. Once inside the warm sanctuary, we shed our coats and gloves and scarves and trotted up the stairs to the choir loft, which was meant to contain only about half our number, so we pressed close together. We chattered and laughed and complained about the cramped space.

Then Mr Leist appeared, and with his look, we fell silent, ready to get to work recording our Christmas album.

"Measure 25: 'Silent Night.'" That resonant voice. We opened our scores. His hand rose. We took a breath and sang from our hearts.

We always sang from deep within—for him. He was stern. He was funny. Unlike anyone else we knew, he expected the best from us, and we met his challenge. Our bodies close, our voices joined, lifting … lifting …

I have never experienced anything so beautiful. Not before. Not since.

Fifty years have passed. Many memories have blurred around the edges. Some have faded away entirely. But those times with the choir, those times with him, endure, remain clearly focused, perhaps because they reside not in my mind but in my heart.

It is time to remember younger days.

The most indelible experiences I had in high school took place while singing with the A Cappella Choir under Mr Leist's direction. In all of my years of education, I never met a teacher who had as profound an effect in shaping my character than he. Whether in class, in rehearsal, or in performance, he set the highest standard of excellence, because he knew we had that excellence within us.

It is uncommon for young people to have, in their lives, an adult who expects and demands only the best from them without compromise. He taught us to learn the notes, meticulously—and then to make music. He taught us not only how to sing, but also how to exceed our own expectations.

What fun we had. What beauty we made.

In anticipation of his ninety-fifth birthday, Mr Leist wrote a book: a guide for young choral directors. Reading it only partially demystified my experience being in A Cappella. There will always be some mystery to those days, and a good deal of magic. For even if young directors learn these lessons well, they will not be able to replicate what Mr Leist did. He was a maestro. For that, one must have something *else*—something deep within that is difficult to put into words. Although, he may have touched upon it when he told me: "When I was teaching, I loved every minute of it." Well, so did we.

Don't get me wrong. He could be sharp. All I needed was to hear only once, when I wasn't paying attention during rehearsal: "Rudoy! You shouldn't have let me hear the choir without you. It sounded good." I never missed a note after that. And then there were the times when he would become exasperated with us, slam his hand down on the top of the rehearsal piano, and call out *"Heiliger Bimbam!"*—the meaning of which, to this day, I have no knowledge.

Rehearsals were long and rigorous and sometimes quite frustrating, especially when Mr Leist began in the middle of a piece at a problematic section that needed work. Rarely would he permit us to sing a whole song from beginning to end. Of course, he had a well-thought-out strategy. He didn't want us to tire of the piece; he wanted it to be fresh in performance, and for us to feel full appreciation of and satisfaction in the music—and therefore he made that experience rare.

We'd occasionally compete against other choirs in state and regional competitions. Hundreds of singers would arrive at an auditorium, and one choir at a time would climb up to the stage and onto the bleachers to sing, while all the others would provide the audience.

One couldn't help but notice that every other choir carried their music and had it in front of them as they performed. We never did. We learned all our music by heart. We had to—in order to focus on Mr Leist. A simple gesture with his index finger could send the sopranos soaring. A pulling together of fingers could end, collectively and uniformly, the tenors' refrain.

Additionally, Mr Leist might change something during performance, and you'd better not have your nose buried in some score and your voice flying out there all by itself when he closed a phrase.

I remember at one competition, during a break, a kid from another choir asked me just what our director was doing up there. From behind, it looked like he wasn't doing anything. I had to laugh. Other directors made large sweeping gestures while they guided their choirs. They had to, in order to draw the singers' attention away from their scores. Mr Leist always directed discreetly, right in front of his body, mostly with his fingers. No flamboyant gestures from this precise director.

The Oshkosh High School A Cappella Choir was first-class. Under Mr Leist's direction over the years, we performed dozens of concerts and musicals in Oshkosh and sang at Madison Square Garden and the 1964 New York World's Fair. We won the praise of our town, our state, and our region, and even had an international reputation, which led to a concert tour of Europe in the summer of 1967. Those facts would suggest that the choir was composed only of fine, elite musicians—but that was not the case. Of course, there were many amongst us who were gifted or trained as singers. But there were others of us—student leaders, athletes, chess players—who were members of the choir. Mr Leist knew what he was doing; he was building a community. He knew that having a number of fine musicians interspersed within the choir would be sufficient: the rest of us would resonate with their voices. And it worked, beautifully.

That trip to Europe was a dream come true for Mr Leist. For eighteen days, the A Cappella Choir under his direction, and the Concert Band under the baton of James Croft, sang and played our way through hundreds of miles of European countryside. It was the culmination of many years of planning and preparation, and an experience that no one who made the trip will ever forget.

We left Oshkosh in two planes on June 12th, transferred to a jet in New York, and arrived in Paris on the 13th. A concert on the Eiffel Tower was our first appearance; the wind blew so hard that the band's scores flew off their stands, but they valiantly played on. Each day was filled with new experiences: Dijon, Milan, Venice (we brought American tourists to tears in Saint Mark's Square), Vienna, city of dreams … We experienced the chill of the Iron Curtain as we crossed into Czechoslovakia, but received a warm reception in Bratislava, where the following day's newspaper reported that "the excellent standard of the Choir and Band conquered the hearts of the listeners present." Then Salzburg, Sankt Florian, Heidelberg, and Rothenburg ob der Tauber.

During those eighteen magical days, we all bonded in ways we had never anticipated, and saw sides of each other previously concealed. Despite what must have been a stressful responsibility corraling over 150 high school students through multiple foreign countries, Mr Leist often seemed relaxed. With his splendid voice, he would lead us in song as our buses made their way from city to city. During those days, it crossed my mind that we not only respected him; we were proud of him, and we adored him.

Mr Leist was an elegant man, full of grace, the exemplar of a gentleman. In his pressed dress slacks and crisp, white shirt, with a trim moustache and a gleaming keychain, he was our David Niven. He was our hero. But not at a distance: he was reserved but never aloof, dignified but never remote.

One autumn, just as we began to rehearse our annual Christmas album, which would later be played in all the brightly lit shops along snowy Main Street as people happily bustled in and out searching for just the right Christmas gifts, Mr Leist discreetly took me aside and told me that he would understand—my being Jewish—if I would prefer not to sing several of the sacred Christmas songs. I was so deeply moved, I doubt I responded with anything nearing my appreciation of his thoughtfulness; probably just, "Oh, that's okay."

Happily, I was able to express my gratitude to him years later for his kindness, not only for that incident, but for his abiding interest and encouragement over the years, like a good, strong wind at my back.

One summer, I was in town on a visit and met up with my pal Steve Verhoeven, also Mr Leist's former student, who had become his dear and faithful friend, golfing partner, and, later, devoted protector. We drove over to Mr Leist's home and picked him up for a run to Leon's drive-in for frozen custard sundaes. This had become a tradition over the years—just a 'guy thing,' as Mr Leist's wife Dorothy always told us to go along without her. I think she knew how important it was for him, and how much he enjoyed the company of former students.

Dorothy. Years later, when she passed away, I wrote to Mr Leist. He wrote back in that distinctly calligraphic handwriting that so suited him: "All references to Dorothy melt in my heart."

On that summer afternoon, we returned from Leon's and sat in the Leists' living room, reminiscing about the old days, complaining about the new days, and talking about family, Mr Leist telling us how much he loved and admired his daughter Sue and his son Fritz. Then he looked at me and said: "I think it's about time for you to call me Fred."

What an astonishing invitation—or, rather, imperative—that was, and what a daunting challenge it presented. But in time, I grew accustomed to it. I'm not sure when admiration turned to friendship, or gratitude to love, but they did. Thanks, Fred.

Fred died at the age of ninety-eight; some angels' choir has a new director. However, as long as memory lasts and choirs sing, he will be here, with those he loved in full measure, and who loved him in return.

Some Things Grow in the Dark

When I was a boy growing up in the 1950s and '60s in a small Midwestern town, children and adolescents were surrounded by images of heterosexual love and relationships on television, in film, onstage, in literature, in magazines, in advertisements. There were no depictions of healthy, happy gay people. Believe me, I searched. Nothing outside me corresponded with something important *inside* me.

Of course, there was the 'fop.' He appeared occasionally in films, and in comic sketches on TV, as a target of derision. My parents would laugh at the *faygeleh*, a Yiddish word that literally means *little bird*, but is pejorative when applied to a gay boy or man. Of course, we are all familiar with the hate-filled terms *fag* and *faggot*; and then there were *queer*, *queen*, *swish*, *fruit*, and *fairy* ... so many words from which to choose to express disdain, revulsion, and disgust.

In junior high school, we gathered in the auditorium for a "hygiene class." The buzz was that it was going to be about sex. I was scared yet hopeful that my secret feelings would be addressed. The class turned out to be mostly about keeping ourselves clean, and being sure to floss—oh, and by the way, this is how babies are made. We each left with a new toothbrush.

In June 1964, the latest issue of *Life* magazine appeared in our mailbox, containing an article titled "Homosexuality in America," which spoke of the "sad and sordid world" of homosexuals, replete with black-and-white photographs showing tough men in leather and tender men in angora. I couldn't find any images of *me*—but I did find plenty of evidence that the orientation of my yearnings was immoral, illegal, and indicative of mental illness. I concluded that it would be best for all concerned to keep my feelings to myself.

Some things grow in the dark: confusion, anxiety, fear, sadness, forbidden longings ... and above all, loneliness. Much like any other teenager, my heart ached for love. Others could demonstrate their romantic attractions and erotic desires; I had to keep mine hidden, private, secret. Instead, I channeled all such energies into service, and became the president of the student council.

I was sort of popular, and did date girls with whom I shared a very meaningful, affectionate affinity … but that's as far as it went. Like all adolescents, I had intense crushes on fellow students, but of necessity had to keep those concealed.

Leaving my hometown and moving to the East Coast for college offered a certain degree of emancipation, but it wasn't until I moved to New York City that I fully came out. Many years earlier, my family had taken our single road trip across the country from Oshkosh to Philadelphia, New York, and Washington, DC. When we were in New York, we visited Greenwich Village, and even as a boy, I felt the *liberation* in that neighborhood and decided then and there: *Someday, I'm going to live here.* And indeed, I did.

Over the years, people have asked: "So, when did you know you were gay?"

My answer is always the same: "Probably about the same time you knew you were straight." For there is no particular mystery about being gay. Despite what some in the media still insist, no human being on this planet has ever made a "choice" to be either straight or gay, and—please, God!—there is no such thing as a "gay lifestyle."

Fifty years later, I wrote to Marcia, a high-school girlfriend of mine:

> In the turmoil of that time, when our bodies were changing and our hearts were awakening and opening bigger than they would ever be again, when we were confused by feelings and alternately overwhelmed by a yearning to be close and a longing for solitude, when we were afraid and lonely, when no one understood us, least of all ourselves, we may have said and done things, and not said and done things, that years later we lament. For me, that period was complicated by the fact that I held deep within a necessary secret. To survive being gay in that period in that town in that family required that I never speak the truth of that aspect of my identity. All of my attractions and desires had to be hidden, for if they were shown, the consequences would have been intolerable. As a result, I lived my life 'as if,' at least to a boundary beyond which I could not go. I regret that in doing so, I may have wounded others in my life, including you. You and I were quite fond of one another, but at a certain point, I

> stepped away, leaving you confused and hurt. For that, I am deeply sorry and now, decades later, I ask your forgiveness.

She responded:

> I will always cherish our time together in those young fragile years. No forgiveness needed. I knew when our paths separated that it wasn't meant to be. I did think of you over the years and always hoped and prayed that you had found love and contentment. At that time in the '60s I was clueless, and my heart now aches that you were so alone with your private pain. I agree that intolerance was the norm during those days, but that doesn't excuse or diminish the turmoil you were experiencing. Please accept my apology on behalf of our class, our families, our community, our Midwest culture for not allowing you to be the person God created you to be. We are the ones in need of forgiveness, and by grace I hope you will give it.

Well, times have changed. The rainbow flag flies. Gay people get married and adopt children. But just beneath the surface of our liberation lies the old hatred that continues to make its defiled appearance in the guise of social commentary, legislation, and revolting religious zealotry.

Know this: there are still young people hiding in the dark.

CO

On Monday evening, 1 December 1969, for the first time since 1942, the Selective Service System of the United States conducted a lottery to determine the order of call to military service. The earlier lottery was for World War II; this one was for the Vietnam War. Along with my friends at Johns Hopkins University in Baltimore, Maryland, I gathered around the television to await the results. As university students, we all had 2-S deferments, but those would end upon graduation. There was much discussion of the war, of military service, of going to Canada.

The call-up would be organized according to date of birth. All the days of the year were printed on slips of paper placed in small, plastic capsules that filled a large glass jar. Capsules were then drawn out of the jar one at a time and opened. The first date drawn was 14 September. The second date drawn was 24 April—my birthdate.

Three months before the lottery, I had requested, from my local Selective Service board back in Wisconsin, the forms necessary to register as a conscientious objector ("CO"). This was a decision preceded by years of sincere reflection and a multitude of conversations with people whom I respected. I wrote to the board that "the basis for my claim of conscientious objection rests on my integral belief in the significance and promise of human life. This is a moral belief to which all else in my life is subordinate and upon which all else in my life is ultimately dependent."

Various people with whom I had had earnest conversations about my decision offered to write letters on my behalf, including the president of a university in Wisconsin; my congressman; the associate dean of undergraduate studies at Johns Hopkins; and my friend Milton S. Eisenhower, that university's former president.

My decision to claim conscientious-objector status was met with intense opposition by my family. I received a four-page letter written on yellow legal pad paper from my father. To him, I was "a coward and a traitor". My mother could not understand why her son, who was so proud of his Cub Scout uniform, who cherished his uncle's

Army jacket, and who, as a boy, had been a competitive marksman, would decide to avoid military service. What they could not accept was that the moral foundation upon which my life rested as a young man imposed a duty of conscience that forbade killing.

Although my decision was firm and incontrovertible, the pressure from others to change it did not subside, and was supplemented by abusive criticism and deeply emotional threats. It took an enormous toll on me in body, mind, and spirit. One evening, I vomited blood. After a series of tests, it was determined that I had developed a bleeding ulcer.

I submitted my claim to the local board. It contained a rather lengthy statement explaining my moral stance and its history of being shaped by my religious upbringing all the way through to my philosophical studies; documentation of my various activities in support of peace; and the letters of support. The board rejected it out of hand, immediately withdrew my student deferment, classified me as 1-A ("REGISTRANT AVAILABLE FOR MILITARY SERVICE"), and ordered me to appear for my physical examination.

I called the secretary of the board, the mother of a dear childhood friend, to ask why my claim had been rejected. She informed me that all CO claims to the local board were rejected initially, on the assumption that the applicant would appeal. I told her I wanted to do so, and she assured me she would begin the paperwork; but I was still required to go for my scheduled physical, which we transferred from Wisconsin to Maryland.

Some time later, I boarded a bus in Baltimore with a group of other apprehensive 1-A young men. We arrived at a gymnasium, where we found doctors sitting at little tables. We lined up until we were called. When I was summoned, I approached the doctor and handed him a medical report that documented my ulcer. He filled out some paperwork and dismissed me.

Shortly thereafter, I received a new draft card that identified me as 4-F ("REGISTRANT NOT QUALIFIED FOR ANY MILITARY SERVICE"). I called the secretary of the local board and asked her about my CO appeal, as I still wanted to pursue it. She told me my case was now closed. But that was not the end of the matter: I now suffered a painful estrangement from my family. It took years, but I built a bridge, brick by brick, back to them.

*

Decades later, when I was taking care of my parents as they made their slow exit offstage, I arrived at their apartment one morning and opened the door to find my ninety-six-year-old father sitting on the living-room sofa. He looked up and smiled: "Oh, are you still here? God bless Dean."

The Copper Bracelet

Back in the early 1970s, a certain kind of copper accessory appeared. It was called a POW/MIA bracelet, and each was engraved with the rank, name, and loss date of an American serviceman captured as a prisoner or missing in action during the Vietnam War. One wore the bracelet to remember them, to feel some connection with them, to hope for their safe return. They cost around three dollars. Approximately five million were distributed.

I wore mine for years, until a crease at the center formed, and it threatened to break in half.

Sometime later, I heard of a special office at the Pentagon that kept track of POW/MIA servicemen. I called and inquired into the fate of the man whose name was engraved on the bracelet I wore. Several minutes passed while files were checked.

"I'm sorry. It's confirmed that he died on 4 November 1969." That was the date engraved on the bracelet in my hand.

"Thank you." I hung up and sat very still for a long time. Although I had been ready to hear this information, I still had that faint hope, which I had carried from the first moment I'd put the bracelet on, so many years earlier.

Years later, I was in Washington, DC and decided to visit the Vietnam Veterans Memorial adjacent to the Lincoln Memorial on The Mall. The sleek, elegant set of two polished, black granite walls forming a V bears the name of every serviceman killed in the war, etched onto each face. I had heard that people could get pencil rubbings of the name they sought. I wanted to pay tribute to Allan.

As I approached the wall, I was expecting to feel a wellspring of emotion … but I did not. This might have had something to do with a busload of kids who had just arrived and were hopping, skipping, and jumping in front of the wall. Clearly, they had not been properly prepared for the significance of the memorial. Time: it passes. The meaning of heartfelt things fades as those who lived through such times disappear from view, and a new generation takes their place.

I went to the book listing all of the names and their locations, and found Allan's. I walked to the section where his name would appear and searched. There it was, high up, but just within reach of my fingertips. I touched it, again expecting some outpouring of emotion. But there was none.

A young Memorial assistant arrived at my side with a little step stool. He had seen me reaching.

"Would you like me to make a rubbing of a name?"

"Yes, please. That one."

With extraordinary care, he made the rubbing of Allan's name. He handed it down to me with great kindness. My fingertips touched his hand. And then, from deep within, as if someone was pulling up a bucket from a well of pain, came the feelings.

I thanked him, walked away, stood under a tree, and wept.

MY PEOPLE

"By and by, I shall look for you, and shall find you everywhere."

Mr Lucky

My father was a lucky man. As a young boy, living in a small *shtetl* south of Kiev, one of his daily responsibilities was to fetch water from the community well at the edge of the village. This required a long walk through the woods. One day, as he wandered through the trees on his way to the well, he spotted a wild tomato plant with three small tomatoes hanging from the stems. Excited by the prospect of bringing something home to feed his parents and himself, he plucked the little fruits, carefully placed them into the pocket of his shirt, and happily continued on his way.

When he arrived at the well, he lowered his bucket, leaning forward to watch its descent into the darkness below. Out of his pocket tumbled the tomatoes. He quickly pulled up the bucket: only water, which he carried home. He kept the experience to himself.

The following day, on his way to the well, he carefully searched the woods for another tomato plant: not a single one. Deeply disappointed, he wandered to the well and lowered his bucket. He heard the splash and then felt the weight of the water as he hauled it up into the light. Bobbing on top were the three small tomatoes.

Another day, on his way to the well, he spied something in the underbrush: a small purse. Inside was a little bit of money and a ring. He proudly presented them to his parents. They sold the ring and bought him his first prayer shawl. Many years later, long after the family had escaped the pogroms and settled in Wisconsin, my grandfather having become a glazier and mirror-maker, my father—then a young man—worked at their little rented space, selling mirrors. It was Christmas, and they had no money and little food. My grandfather told my father to go to the shop and sit there in case a customer came in.

"But it's Christmas Eve. No one is going to come."

"Go."

My father went and sat in the shop, alone and silent, as snow fell in the darkness. Suddenly, around 11 PM, a woman, seeing the shop's light, rushed in. She looked around frantically; all she saw was my father, and a single mirror hanging on the wall.

"Is that mirror for sale?"

"Yes."

"I'll buy it!"

And so my father closed up shop and took the money home to his parents' surprise and delight.

Time passed. When my father was older, with a business of his own and married, he and my mother took a trip to California. They drove all the way from Wisconsin without a spare tire. When they arrived, my father went to the racetrack. As he stood in line to make a bet, the man ahead of him placed his; as he turned and walked past my father, he looked directly at him and told him to place a bet on a particular horse. My father recognized the man—it was the actor Don Ameche. He placed the bet, and won. Several days later, they returned to Wisconsin, with a spare tire in the trunk.

Some years later, my folks were in Las Vegas, staying at a fancy hotel on the Strip. They had just seen a show with Harry Belafonte and wandered into the casino, where my father headed to the craps table. He started betting, and started losing. Suddenly, Harry Belafonte appeared behind my father and asked him how he was doing.

"Not so good."

"Your luck will change, now that I'm here." And, indeed, it did. My father cashed in a lot of chips that evening.

Decades later, Harry and I were serving together on the Board of Directors of the Robert F. Kennedy Memorial. During a break in one of our meetings, as we gathered at a table for coffee and sandwiches, I told Harry that story.

"So, that's how you got through college."

"Yes, Harry. And by the way, thanks."

Of course, my father's best luck was meeting my mother. Ed and Belle married in 1944. When she passed away in the summer of 2007, he was lost. A short while later, she called him to her side.

Although never particularly inclined to take risks or gamble, I, too, have had good fortune: Ed was my dad.

Something More to Learn / Something More to Teach

My father, then ninety-seven, and I were sitting on the sofa in the living room of my folks' Florida apartment, reminiscing. I suppose I had heard the story he was telling dozens of times before, but he was a good storyteller and sometimes would surprise me with a new embellishment of history. He finished. We laughed. And then he just fell silent, staring at the carpet.

"What's up, Dad?"

"Why am I still alive?"

You know how after a conversation—hours or days later—you think of what you *should* have said? This time, who knows why, I said just the right thing: "Because you have something more to learn, or something more to teach."

He looked at me and sat up a bit. "Maybe you're right."

Most often, when faced with someone else's sorrow, I end up sympathizing—*feeling for*—which, despite whatever good intentions I may have, ends up with that person's truest feelings either being dismissed or explained away. But in this moment, through some good fortune, I had slipped into empathy—*feeling with*. My father felt seen, and heard.

In the rock opera *Tommy* by The Who, the main character calls out several times during the story: *"See me. Feel me. Touch me. Heal me."* When I teach, I tell my students to learn their personality theories well, and their therapy techniques by heart, and all the significant differences that distinguish and define human beings. But, I also tell them, know that whomever sits before you yearns for the *same* things: to be seen beneath the mask they wear, to have someone feel along with them what they are feeling, to be touched, and to be healed.

When I was in training at Bellevue, my most astute and insightful supervisor, Walter Kass, told me that if you hold a tuning fork in each hand, strike one, and bring the other close to the one vibrating, the second will begin to resonate, too. That's empathy. It won't work if the second tuning fork is bound in cloth.

Somehow, when my father questioned his existence, I felt what he was feeling and instead of retreating in defense against the power of his question, unbound, I spoke the truth.

I do not know what more my father had to learn in the last few months of his life, but I know he had more to teach—about patience and understanding and compassion and acceptance. I know, because I was his student.

No Fear. No Regrets.

Toward the end of her life, my mother, then ninety-two, and I were sitting out on the balcony of my parents' Florida apartment on a typically hot, humid summer afternoon, smoking cigarettes.

"So, Mom, what's it like, this last chapter?" I asked. We had a habit of speaking frankly.

She took a long drag and thought for awhile: "No fear. No regrets."

My mother was a woman of remarkable restraint. Not remarkable to her; remarkable to me. She was one of those people who are naturally able to speak the truth in just a few words. I am not.

I took her answer at face value. She had no fear of dying, and had no regrets about the life she had lived. Several weeks later, she stopped speaking. She still had the ability to talk, but decided that she had nothing more to say. Instead, she just smiled a lot. A few months later, she passed away.

Several months afterward, as I awoke one morning, it crossed my mind that in answering the question, my mother was not only speaking of her own life, but giving me an instruction for mine. Looking back, I am ashamed of having done some things and said some things, and have regrets about things I didn't do, things I didn't say, because I was afraid—of failure, of revealing my inadequacies, of success, and facing its responsibilities. In every instance, the moment was lost, the opportunity passed.

If life were a straight line, we'd see what's just up ahead, and prepare for it. But the road bends, and branches. It takes some grace to walk the stretch we're on, making choices along the way. We are given only moments to live—not days or years; moments. And *every* moment, every step on that road, is new and filled with promise, fulfilled if we have the courage. Though the past might contain regret, the present need not, nor the future.

Onward. No fear. No regrets.

Bound to Obey

When my folks were in their eighties, I flew to Florida and cheerfully presented them with a stack of colorful brochures for assisted-living facilities—in Wisconsin, where family resided; in New Mexico, where I lived; and in Florida itself.

"No thanks. We want to stay home."

By the time they were in their nineties, it was becoming clear that some form of assistance would be necessary in order for them to live safely. On one of my visits, the phone rang in their apartment. I picked up. It was a woman named Yvonne, who told me that for years she had helped various residents in my parents' apartment building as they approached their later years, and that the staff of the building had informed her that my folks might have such a need. I thanked her and took her number, saying "not yet."

A couple of days later, I arrived at the apartment to say goodbye before flying back to New Mexico. My mom was in the kitchen.

"Hi, where's Dad?"

"Oh, he's still in bed."

It was already the middle of the morning, and that concerned me; I went into their bedroom. Dad was lying there, disoriented and disheveled. I got him out of bed, cleaned up, into a robe, and out onto the living-room sofa. I canceled my flight, called Yvonne, and arranged for her to meet me at the apartment later in the afternoon.

I took my mom out onto the balcony, and we sat at the table. "Mom, it's time to get some help."

She stared at me and slammed her hand down on the glass table. "No strangers!"

"Mom, I want to keep you and Dad safe. Just a little bit of help."

She softened. That afternoon, I met Yvonne at the elevator, introduced myself, and explained the situation. She understood. "I want you to know that, if you hire me, I will be with your parents until they cross over," she said.

We walked into the apartment, and both my parents smiled. They recognized Yvonne from her work helping some of their friends. I hired her to come in every day for just a couple of hours. As time went by, those hours were extended, and eventually I hired two more nurses so that my folks had care around the clock.

For almost two years, I flew back and forth from New Mexico to Florida every two weeks. Every time I arrived at my parents' door, I would pause to prepare myself. Although I was in constant touch with Yvonne, who assured me that all was well, I knew that seeing my folks slowly disappear was going to be challenging each time.

Friends had told me that old people become like children. Well, sort of … but with children, one can see a future in which they will grow up. With elders, one can only see a future without them.

Given my travel schedule, I stopped practicing and teaching. There were times when I awoke and lay in bed, not knowing exactly where I was. My commitment to my parents defined my life. Some saw it as a burden; I saw it as my birthright. When friends praised me for my virtuous dedication, I would reply, "Thanks … but an act of virtue requires that one make a choice. I have no choice. I do what I do out of love and duty in equal measure."

In the second year of their care, my mom passed away while Yvonne was brushing her hair. I happened, at that time, to be in New Mexico, and immediately flew out to be with my dad. During that visit, I took Yvonne out onto the balcony, and told her: "You have been so devoted to my folks. Please know, from my heart, how much I appreciate your taking care of people I love. I know that many times, when my father has been difficult at night, the nurse would call you and you would get out of bed and get dressed and drive back here and calm him down and sleep on the floor next to his bed. How could you do these things?"

"Where I am bound, I must obey," she replied.

"Bound? What do you mean?"

"When we met, I told you I would be with your parents until they crossed over. I gave you my word."

Who talks like that? Angels, I think.

Six weeks later, my dad died. At his funeral, during my eulogy, I explained why he waited: "I think Mom wanted some time alone after sixty-three years." Everyone laughed, including—I truly believe I heard them—Belle and Ed.

Looking back, that chapter informed my heart, broke it, and healed it. I am a better person, a better man, as a result—and I wouldn't have missed a moment of it, not for all the world.

Looking for Signs

The day my mom died, I went outside after being on the phone continuously with family and the funeral agency. The sun was low in the western sky. After a remarkable thunder-and-lightning storm, the colors were vibrant and the desert smelled green. I stood there, away from the house, and said: "Mom, I hope you see this now."

Then I heard something up above. A magnificent hawk flew toward me from the northwest. When he got to me, he made a circle high over my head, then headed east. It was a breathtaking moment. I know that, at times such as these, we tend to look for signs. I also know that there are signs everywhere, all the time. But this felt different. She was near.

That night, mourning my loss, I got into bed in my darkened room, having forgotten to turn the bathroom light off. I noticed that a shaft of light was coming from there, spreading out and dissolving the darkness in the room. But there was no equal shaft of darkness from the bedroom going into the bathroom. Light overcomes darkness.

The following day, I flew to Florida to be with my dad, who was now alone after more than six decades. I found him sitting on the sofa, disconsolate. He looked up at me.

"She's gone."

"Yes."

"She was sitting right here, and just stopped breathing."

Having heard a different story from their nurse, I said: "No, Dad, she passed while Yvonne was brushing her hair."

He screamed: "Why are you saying that!"

Immediately, but too late, I realized that I had violated his necessary revision of the story in order to place his beloved wife next to him when she slipped away.

"I'm so sorry, Dad."

The morning after I returned home from visiting my dad, I walked outside to find a bank of wild, white flowers spread beneath a tree. At that time, I had lived in the desert for eighteen years, and I had never before seen these flowers.

Shortly afterward, my father died. A couple of months passed. I had not yet cried. And then, one day, while doing the dishes, I started to weep into the sink.

The loss of one's parents is unlike any other. They nurtured me, protected me, encouraged me, and consoled me. And now my heart was filled with sadness and gratitude.

There is nothing so full as a broken heart.

They were near.

Into Debt to Give

Sixty years ago, my dad observed that the kids in my hometown of Oshkosh didn't have much to do. He decided we needed a YMCA. He knew that buying the land and constructing the facility was going to cost a lot of money, so he got down to it.

Wisely bypassing all the politics of the town, he arranged a series of one-on-one lunches with fellow executives from local businesses to discuss the project. Those were the days of three-martini lunches. During the meal, he and his guest would discuss this and that, and then, over coffee, he would say: "I'm sure you agree with me that the kids of this town need something to do. For example, the only pool is at the country club, and the vast majority of kids' families aren't invited to join—and if they were, they couldn't afford it." The guest would nod in agreement. "I've been in touch with YMCA National, and we are exploring the idea of building a 'Y' here. Good idea, right?"

Again, the nodding. Then my dad would reach into his suit coat pocket (everyone wore suits in those days) and pull out a card, showing one side of it to his guest and, pointing to a dollar amount written on it, say: "This is what I'm giving." Eyes would widen. Then he would turn the card around and add: "And this is what you're giving."

Dad's boldness of vision and conduct paid off. The land was bought and the "Y" was built, and the first president of the Oshkosh Community Young Men's Christian Association was my father—a Jew.

The beauty of a small town.

*

When my father died, I was faced with the responsibility of writing his obituary. How in the world was I going to encapsulate ninety-seven years of a person's life? I decided I would simply write one thing that I wanted people to know about him: he went into debt to give money away.

This started when, as a young man, he took out a loan from a bank to buy a small business. He had no business history, no collateral …

only his word and his ambition. This was back in the day when you sat down with a banker, and, if he liked you and trusted you, you got a loan. Every month, my dad would take out his ledger, place a ruler on a line, and draw through that month's loan payment with a red pencil. After some time, he returned to the bank to request another loan.

"Ed, your business is doing well and your payments are always on time. Why do you need another loan?"

"I need more money," Dad replied, "so I can give it away."

He got the loan. And thus began decades of gifts to countless charities. I asked my father once why he was willing to go further into debt to give money away.

"When my parents, sister, and I were escaping the Russian pogroms, making our way in the dark of night through forests and farmlands, we were hidden by strangers across Europe—courageous Jews and righteous Gentiles. They risked their lives helping us. I will never know who they were, but I am under an obligation to help others for the rest of my life to honor them."

I wanted people to know that about him. In the fifty-eight years I knew him, it was perhaps the most important lesson he taught me, and his most enduring legacy.

My father's story, like those of so many Jewish immigrants who escaped the antisemitic violence and oppression of Eastern Europe, is both heroic and inspiring. My life, and the lives of my entire family, have been a cakewalk by comparison because of his generosity to us. But that was his intent, and his gift.

My father realized the American Dream. Yet, beneath the surface of his outstanding accomplishments, what motivated him? Years after his harrowing experiences as a boy, even in the safety of a new country filled with opportunity, he was driven to overcome the haunting memories of his youth. My father escaped the pogroms, but he never stopped running.

Michail

Following the passing of my parents, I began to search for someone whose identity I did not know. From my computer in the New Mexico desert, I searched the website of the United States Holocaust Memorial Museum in Washington, DC, which maintains a database of survivors of the Holocaust, and that of Yad Vashem in Jerusalem, which maintains a database of those who perished. I was reaching across space and time for my family—to those who suffered, and those who were lost. I found branches of my family tree that had been severed by the brutality of the Nazis and their accomplices. I found individual stories of precious lives ended by the grotesque hatred that flourished across Europe during World War II. I read and grieved, and read and grieved. And then I came upon the story of Michail Rudoy.

In the autumn of 1941, German forces swept across Ukraine; on 19 September they captured and occupied the capital, Kiev. On 26 September, the military governor made the decision to exterminate the Jews of Kiev. The *Einsatzgruppen*—SS killing squads—were brought in to accomplish the task. The order was posted throughout the city:

> *All the Yids of the city of Kiev and its vicinity must appear on Monday September 29, 1941 by 8 AM at the corner of Melnikova and Dokhterivskaya streets (next to the cemetery). Bring documents, money and valuables, and also warm clothing, bed linen, etc. Any Yids who do not follow this order and are found elsewhere will be shot.*" [Source: Yad Vashem, The World Holocaust Remembrance Center, Jerusalem.]

That Monday, over 30,000 Jews from Kiev and the surrounding villages gathered by the cemetery, expecting to be loaded onto trains for resettlement. The enormous crowd of men, women, and children could not have known what was to happen. They were marched to Babi Yar, a ravine just outside the city, and there, over a two-day period of uninterrupted executions, were murdered by a special team of SS units supported by other German troops and local collaborators.

In later testimony, Fritz Höfer, a German eyewitness who had been a truck driver in *Sonderkommando 4a*, described the scene:

> *... Once undressed they were led into the ravine which was about 150 meters long and 30 meters wide and a good 15 meters deep ... When they reached the bottom of the ravine they were seized by members of the Schutzpolizei and made to lie down on top of Jews who had already been shot ... The corpses were literally in layers. A police marksman came along and shot each Jew in the neck with a submachine gun ... I saw these marksmen stand on layers of corpses and shoot one after the other ... The marksmen would walk across the bodies of the executed Jews to the next Jew, who had meanwhile lain down, and shoot him.* [Michael Berenbaum, *The World Must Know*, United States Holocaust Memorial Museum (2006), pp. 97-98.]

According to the *Einsatzgruppen's* "Operational Situation Report," 33,771 Jews from Kiev and its vicinity were systematically executed at Babi Yar on 29-30 September 1941, on the eve of Yom Kippur, the Jewish Day of Atonement, in what was to be the largest single massacre in the history of the Holocaust.

Had my father, his sister, and his parents not been able to escape the pogroms from their village outside of Kiev years earlier in 1922, they, too, would have been murdered. Amongst dozens of my relatives listed by Yad Vashem was Michail Rudoy, son of Beniamin and Makhlya. He was seventeen years old when he was murdered at Babi Yar.

Reading of the death of this boy, I vowed to think of him every day for the rest of my life. But given the many distractions of this existence, how was I to be reminded? I looked at my arm and saw his name, in the place where the Nazis branded my people.

*

I had never had a tattoo, and knew nothing about the process of getting one. A few days later, I began my search along old Route 66 in Albuquerque, where I knew I would find several tattoo studios.

Those who know me know my usual wardrobe: pressed khaki trousers and a starched oxford cloth shirt. When I entered these establishments and met the eyes of the young, tattooed, and pierced artists, I could read their astonishment and amusement at the appearance of this middle-aged man. But these were to be my teachers, and when I explained that I wanted a tattoo on my arm of the name of a person I wanted to remember, they responded to my earnestness and were most helpful in describing the process I would go through.

After visiting a half-dozen studios, I found one in which I felt immediately comfortable. There was a pretty receptionist at the desk with an intricate, multicolored tattoo from her fingertips to her shoulder, and a young fellow sitting cross-legged on the desk eating a sandwich.

"I'd like to get a tattoo," I said, showing him the Hebrew letters I had printed out on a sheet.

"I can help you with that."

He ran the paper through a kind of copying machine and out came a print on a transparent sheet, with the Hebrew letters in blue powder on the back. We went to his room, and I sat down on the chair. He asked where I wanted the tattoo; I pointed to the place on my forearm. He positioned the sheet and patted it, leaving behind a powdered blue template.

"Is that about right?"

"Yes."

"Can I ask what this is?"

"I'd like to explain it to you when we're done."

"Cool."

With great care, he began the work—interestingly, starting the tattoo from the right, at the beginning of Michail's name (Hebrew is read from right to left). In about twenty minutes, we were done. He lay some plastic wrap on my arm and taped it down.

"Keep this on there for a day or two, because the ink will bleed out for a while." I stood up, and we faced one another. "Can you tell me now what this is?"

"This is the name of Michail Rudoy, a cousin of mine who perished in the Holocaust. He was seventeen."

His eyes filled with tears. We stood in silence.

"What's up?" I asked.

"I'm German," he replied. "During the war, half my family left Germany to get away from Hitler, and the other half stayed and became complicit. This helps me to make amends."

We reached toward one another and held on. I had thought getting the tattoo would change my life; what I didn't know was that, first, it would change another's.

The Atonement Tree

It was time to get off the world and onto the Earth.

Having had enough of telephones and emails and video calls, I put on my sneakers, grabbed a walking stick, and started on a hike down the hill toward the creek to visit a favorite cottonwood tree, which had turned gold in the October air.

It was Yom Kippur, the highest of all holy days in the Jewish calendar—the Day of Atonement, a moment in time for reconciliation and renewal. As I walked down the hill, I did my best to leave behind my various preoccupations. Within a few minutes, my senses opened, and I was more present to what surrounded me: the green cedar smell of the desert, the huge, blue vaulted sky, the soft sand beneath my feet.

I heard him before I saw him. *Whoosh, whoosh, whoosh.* Slowly, from high above, a raven flew down toward me. I stood still. He came very close. Just before flying up into the sky again, he pushed the air beneath his wing against my cheek. These sorts of things happen in the desert occasionally. Actually, they happen all the time. We just need to be there when they do.

Onward, to the tree. Along the way, I spied a bright, white stone in the sand, perfectly smooth. I picked it up and rolled it between my fingers. Then: into my pocket.

Even their name is instructive. Like us, the leaves of the cottonwood tree begin bright and filled with promise. Then, in the autumn of their lives, they let go of their attachments and entrust themselves to the cleansing wind, float, and come down to earth, having at last shown their true colors. And then they leave.

I arrived at the tree, its bright yellow leaves clattering in the breeze like pieces of dry parchment. Many had already fallen from the branches, but most of those had already begun to turn brown. I did find a handful still pristine, and gathered them up in my handkerchief. Turning to leave, it crossed my mind that I wanted more. I searched, but found none on the ground that had not already begun to turn. I looked up. There were perfect leaves still on the branches. I pulled at one, but it resisted. Using two hands, I plucked it off. Sap from the leaf's stem dripped on to my fingers and down into the palm of my hand.

Shame is a powerful emotion; not just guilt for having *done* something wrong, but shame at *being* something wrong. In that moment, I was ashamed. In my desire for more, I did not wait patiently for a gift. I took it. The tree did not judge me. Judgment came from deep within myself. The only right thing to do, having done something wrong, is to make amends. I apologized to the cottonwood.

As I stood beneath the sheltering tree, the significance of the day became clear. Atonement—to be at one with everything—is both a promise and an imperative. It requires of us a thoughtful intention that engages both mind and heart. It demands of us to pause before we speak or act, to consider the Buddhist inquiry, *what will this further?* If our speech or action furthers the fracturing of Creation, we ought not to do it. If it furthers the healing of an already too-divided world, then that, we should do.

My Navajo friend Wind once taught me the tradition of giving with my right hand and receiving with my left. That completes the circle. There is no *taking*.

With gratitude for the lessons learned, I reached into my pocket and, with my right hand, placed the perfect, white stone at the base of the Atonement Tree.

*

September 2021 marked the eightieth anniversary of the death of my young cousin Michail Rudoy, whose name is tattooed on my left forearm. He died eight years before I was born. Having no memory or photograph of him, I have had to construct an image and a life. When I think of him—especially when I stand under the stars and offer prayers up to Whomever might be listening—I imagine what fear he must have experienced when the Nazis murdered him at the ravine called Babi Yar.

I knew I wanted to honor him in some way. I decided to hike down to the creek, where I have always found comfort, solace, and answers. Two weeks after Yom Kippur, on the warm, sunlit morning of Wednesday, 29 September, I headed out across the desert toward the Atonement Tree.

I was accompanied by a group of ravens high up in the sky, who seemed to know where I was going. As is so often the case when I make this hike, my preoccupations eventually drifted away, and my senses opened. I stopped several times to rain birdseed on anthills; the occupants scurried back and forth, gathering supplies for the coming winter. I thought of Michail, but nothing in particular came to mind.

There was the tree, some distance away. Someone was behind me. I looked. There was no one … and yet, I felt a presence. I continued on, knowing that Michail was following me. By the time we arrived, he was beside me. We walked around the Atonement Tree to where the creek runs. I got down on my knees to watch and listen. By now, Michail was within me, watching through my eyes, listening through my ears. After a while, I rose and began the hike home.

We walked by a grove of cottonwoods, their autumn leaves now turned bright yellow. The air was still. It crossed my mind that I would have liked to have taken all those we lost at Babi Yar to this peaceful place.

At that moment, a breeze swept across the desert. Thousands of leaves shimmered silently under the sun.

Daniel, My Friend for Life

It took me many years before I was able to visit the United States Holocaust Memorial Museum. I traveled to Washington, DC quite often, and could have gone, but I avoided it. Having grown up with indelible stories and images of the Holocaust, I simply didn't want my heart broken again.

And then one day, I went.

As I walked in, I didn't know quite where to go, how to begin. I saw a group of schoolkids with their teacher, and decided to follow them. They entered an exhibit titled *Remember the Children: Daniel's Story*, which presents the narrative of one family's experiences during the Holocaust from the perspective of a boy growing up in Nazi Germany—from the first anti-Jewish laws to ghetto exile to deportation to a concentration camp. Throughout the rooms depicting where he lived over those years, there are, on the walls, enlarged pages from his diary describing his life as these events unfolded. His clothing hangs in a closet.

Unlike other memorials in Washington, where I have often witnessed children running and playing with no knowledge or appreciation of the meaning of where they are, these children were silent and attentive as we walked through Daniel's story. Their teacher had prepared them, and the quiet exhibit itself commanded their attention and respect.

When we exited, we entered a brightly lit room with low tables and chairs and bulletin boards covering the walls. The kids were invited to sit at the tables, and were provided with index cards and crayons with which to draw and write messages to Daniel and then post them on the walls. One such card depicted a boy standing behind barbed wire, inscribed by a child with the following printed words: DANIEL, MY FRIEND FOR LIFE.

The enormity of the Holocaust is too inconceivable for the mind to contain. But the story of one boy can be held in memory. Over the years, I have often thought of Daniel and, in a way, he has visited me on occasion.

Grief has a life of its own. Like all living things, it yearns for attention; like an insistent child pulling at your garments, it sometimes arrives at the most inopportune time. But if it were a child, you would set everything else aside for a moment to comfort it and, being comforted, it would go to sleep for a while, perhaps until tomorrow.

Certain cherished things in this life are immeasurable. We don't become fully aware of that until we lose them. One and a half million of the six million whom we lost were children. They moved out of form and out of suffering. Too soon, before they could even wave goodbye, they slipped through a portal into the eternal present moment—where we are all headed, all along—no longer contained within space and time, no longer caught between memory and anticipation. And that is where they freely reside. There is no past or future where they are, where all are whom we have lost. They are patient, awaiting our arrival.

In the meantime, when my heart is seized by sorrow, what am I to do? How am I to honor these children, my children?

It is said amongst my people that when God created the universe, it was One. He then breathed His *ruach*, His breath, into His creation. It shattered into billions and billions of pieces, not able to contain the great spirit of the Lord. It was then that He created human beings and gave voice to our paramount responsibility, *tikkun olam*: heal, repair, and transform the world, gather the pieces together, do not further fracture Creation.

When those precious to us disappear from view, when we wonder what we can do—when we are haunted by the thought that whatever we do is never enough, for how can it be enough—our duty is clearly before us.

We are here. This is what we know. Every act of goodness is unending. Every decent deed changes the world. When, in our hearts, we dedicate these to them, when we do these things for them, we fulfill our duty on their behalf; in those moments, we extend their lives through ours.

My children, by and by, I shall look for you, and shall find you everywhere.

IN MY CARE

"They held it all in memory, as do I."

Tommy

While reading the newspaper in my Greenwich Village apartment one frigid winter day in early January 1978, I came across an ad for therapeutic counselors at a residential summer camp for emotionally disturbed children and adolescents in upstate New York. As I was in graduate school studying for my doctorate in clinical psychology, I thought this might be a fruitful use of my summer off from studies.

I submitted my application and was accepted into the group of a couple dozen counselors. We met every week in the city to bond and to learn about the protocols of the camp. As summer approached, we were sitting in a circle in the basement of a community center, and the director of the camp, Steve, asked us each to speak about any hesitations we had regarding what lay ahead. When my turn came, I simply said: "I really don't have any. I'm ready."

There was a long pause. Looking directly at me, Steve said, "We'll wait."

I sat there, all eyes on me. The hot seat. Then, I blurted out: "I can't throw a ball. Never learned how. When I've tried, it always ends up going wild or landing just a few feet in front of me. I guess I don't know when to let it go. There are ball sports at camp, and I'm sure I'm going to make a fool of myself."

"Dean, many of the kids at camp don't know how to throw a ball, and are frightened to try, having been humiliated in the past. If you can show them that you're okay with that, despite your own difficulties, it will be enormously beneficial to them."

That's how good this guy was.

Well, the summer came, and all the counselors arrived at camp a week before the children to set everything up. On the day of the kids' arrival, a station wagon peeled into the parking area and came to a sudden stop, sand flying from the tires. Several counselors surrounded the car to unload the footlocker strapped to the roof. The father inside leaned across his young son, opened his door, and sort of pushed him out. Once the boy and the cargo were free of the car, the father drove off. I was pretty stunned by that, but later came to understand.

Tommy was seven years old and suffered severe autism. He had no expressive speech. He did talk, but only in the form of echolalia: "Tommy, this is a ball." His response—*"Tommy, this is a ball"*—spoken in exactly the same cadence and tone.

Tommy was unusually beautiful. He was slight, fine-featured, and had a headful of dark curls; he was the kind of child people wanted to pet. However, he could not tolerate being touched. In fact, if anyone came close to him and he had no exit, he would jump on them and bite them, hard. After a few days at camp, no one wanted to approach him, lest they be attacked. Tommy was left most of the day to his own devices, sitting under a big tree, where he flipped his shoelaces back and forth.

As I had a bit more experience than most of the counselors, I was assigned to work with the adolescents. However, every day we were given an hour off just to unwind. I asked Steve if I could spend my hour with Tommy. He agreed.

When I first approached Tommy, sitting under the tree, I started telling him a story about the birds on the branches. We made no eye contact, and it appeared that he was unaware or at least indifferent to my presence. When I was about twenty feet away, I noticed he began to tense up. So I sat down in the grass and continued with my story.

As the days went by, Tommy permitted me to get closer. By "permitted," I mean he allowed me nearer before tensing up. It took about a week, but eventually we were sitting side by side under the tree, all the while with me telling him stories.

Upon seeing me sitting next to Tommy, other counselors would come by. When they were within twenty feet, Tommy would grab my arm and gently bite it. I would tell the counselors to sit down in the grass where they were, and that if they wanted to come closer, they would need to earn Tommy's trust. That was a lot of effort … and no one took up the challenge.

Tommy and I sort of became pals. We spent an hour a day together, and sometimes I would sit next to him at mealtimes to keep him calm. Although he had no speech, he did know a bit of sign language. He knew the letter P—which, when he made the sign, meant he had to pee. However, he never demonstrated the sign directly in front of him: he would just make it. You had to be on the lookout. One day, he made the sign with his hand at his side. I caught sight of it and asked him if he needed to pee. He nodded his head, and we went to the bathroom. He stood at the toilet and peed into the bowl. Then, smiling, he looked at me and slowly turned; the arc of his pee splashed onto the floor.

"Tommy, I expect better behavior from you," I said. His smile vanished and he returned to the bowl. Actually, I was amused by his mischief and considered that his little joke bonded us in a new way.

As with all the kids at camp, by the second month Tommy had unfolded his wings a bit. In fact, if anyone had visited midway through the summer, many would not even have known that this was a therapeutic camp for emotionally disturbed children. However, over the final two weeks, things began to unravel.

Every night, after putting the kids to bed, the counselors would meet to debrief. Steve alerted us to what we would experience in the last two weeks: "The kids know they are going to have to go home soon. You're going to see some dramatic acting out and decompensation in their behavior. They have difficulty putting words to their feelings. Goodbyes are very difficult for them. You will see rage, and it will be directed at you personally."

He was right, and it was painful.

On one of our last nights together, I was sitting next to Tommy at dinner. He wouldn't eat. Suddenly, he picked up his plate and threw it into the air. Even he seemed shocked at his behavior. Then he grabbed my arm and bit into it, hard. Other counselors ran to the table, restrained him, and began cleaning up. I excused myself, left the dining hall, and went outside to sit on the bench. All sorts of complicated feelings began to surface. Steve came out and stood behind me. He didn't say a word, but when he placed his hand on my shoulder, I broke down.

Camp ended, and the cars arrived to pick up the kids—including the station wagon. I had come to understand that father. Tommy was probably difficult to live with, and required a great deal of patient attention. Maybe there were other children in the family. In any case, the father was probably relieved to drop Tommy off at camp, knowing he would be cared for, and that his family might now have a quiet summer. I understood.

Tommy taught me more than anyone I have ever met about respecting personal space and boundaries. And the children's enraged behavior toward the end of the season became understandable: they had grown, but now needed to shrink, in order to fit back into their family puzzles.

I also came to understand the unbridled excitement that so many of the returning campers had shown on that first day of arrival, at the beginning of the summer. They *remembered* how good it was to be there. They held it all in memory, as do I.

Bellevue

During my doctoral studies, I served an internship at the New York University–Bellevue Medical Center from 1979–81. It was a prized placement, with only six openings and hundreds of applications. I believe I won the spot because they knew me already: several years earlier, I had volunteered for a year on the Child Inpatient Ward, working with autistic children. Apparently I'd left a positive impression, and they welcomed me back.

I have many stories about Bellevue. Here are four.

*

During my first year, I worked both sides of the hyphen, seeing patients at University Hospital (a private facility) and at Bellevue Hospital (which is public). That juxtaposition in and of itself was eye-opening. No matter their place in the socio-economic strata, all the patients faced the same kinds of life challenges. All struggled with fear and sadness. All had hopes and regrets, and yearned for meaning.

One of my Bellevue patients was a middle-aged Black man who, for years, had suffered clinical depression and paranoia. Although a trained engineer who had been employed by a multinational company, he could no longer work as a result of his disability and received Supplemental Security Income (SSI). At the time I knew him, the administration of President Ronald Reagan had cut back such benefits. My patient arrived one afternoon, panicked by a letter notifying him that he would no longer receive his monthly check. I had to think fast, as this issue seemed beyond the perimeter of our therapeutic work.

He had no other resources. I told him I would represent him. "For us to do this together," I said, "we will need to go through your hospital record. There may be things in it that might make you uncomfortable."

"You mean that I've been diagnosed with depression and paranoia? No problem."

And so we set to work with his psychiatric file; I wrote a summary, and we went to court, both wearing jackets and ties out of respect for the proceedings. We were called to the bench, where I handed the judge my paper. He instructed us to have a seat at a long table. Then he read my report—every word—and looked up.

"The Court finds for the plaintiff, and orders that all his SSI benefits be restored."

That was that. My patient asked if he could buy me a cup of coffee. Having already 'violated' what I had learned about professional boundaries, I said yes, and we walked over to a coffee shop and talked about our experience.

That changed our relationship. I had proven something to him about my commitment to his well-being; I had earned his trust in a new way.

Some weeks later, he came in for our appointment and told me that, as he was shaving that morning and looking in the mirror, the thought crossed his mind: *Who will be afraid of me today?* His experience of being a Black man in our society awakened and informed me, and broke something in my heart. As with so many of my patients over the years, I am deeply grateful for the lessons I learned from him.

*

During that first internship year, I was rotated every three months to a different inpatient service. Once I found myself back at the Children's Ward, where I had volunteered years earlier. Most of the children lived at the hospital Monday through Friday, going home on weekends. There was a little autistic boy there with whom I worked. During the week he seemed occasionally to reach beyond his private world. At first, he would play only by himself, but by Friday he was playing with others. However, it was not uncommon that, when his parents returned him to the ward on Monday, he would be deeply withdrawn. Sometimes we would notice bruises.

We arranged a home visit and discovered that the father was an alcoholic and out of work, and that the mother was moderately intellectually disabled. They had only minimal social interaction with others. When their son returned home after a week at the hospital, he would be "overactive," which they couldn't handle. They put him under an overturned crib, where he would remain throughout the weekend.

At our next case conference, under the guidance of a social worker, we developed a family plan. We got the father into Alcoholics Anonymous and job training, and engaged the mother with a support group of other mothers of autistic children. Those interventions were remarkably fruitful. The boy continued to improve. I learned from that experience not only that social workers are often the least applauded members of a psychiatric team within a hospital—whose hierarchy is top-heavy with MDs and PhDs—but also that every patient lives within concentric circles of family and society. If, in our treatments, we change their shape, they will no longer fit into the puzzle in which they reside. They will often be pounded back into a shape that fits. Therefore we are compelled to open the frame of both our understanding and our work—and address the puzzle itself.

*

There was another boy with whom I worked as an outpatient, across the street at University Hospital. He was brought in with a diagnosis of Obsessive-Compulsive Disorder. The paramount symptom that had led to this determination was the fact that, every night, he would get up several times to check the lock on his family's apartment door. In our play therapy together, his fantasies of intrusion and feared violence were manifest. Upon interviewing his parents, I learned that there had been break-ins in the neighborhood. It became clear that the boy's concerns, revealed in his secret nightly rituals, were not the result of an intrapsychic problem, but rather his understandable fears for the safety of his family. From that point forward, I decided not to work with the boy individually, but with the whole family. That work proved successful, as the parents were able to acknowledge that there had indeed been a local problem, and assure their son that now everything was safe and sound. Once again, I was reminded of the importance of seeing my patients not as isolated from their environment, but as part of, and responsive to, their surrounds. I was also made aware of the sometimes myopic nature of psychiatric diagnoses, which can fail to take into account the *context* of a person's life.

*

After my first year of internship ended, I was asked to remain for a second year as Chief Intern Psychologist, with an appointment to the faculty of NYU's School of Medicine. This was an unprecedented honor. NYU-Bellevue had never offered a second-year psychology internship before. They also said that, in addition to my outpatient work, I would no longer rotate through inpatient services, but could choose one in which to stay for the entire duration. I chose the adolescent ward.

When I started that second year, I was given full responsibility for one of the kids there. Mark had been picked up on the street for hustling and doing drugs. He was a "Bellevue Kid," having been born at the hospital and treated there all his life. The police in the city knew a lot of these kids; rather than treat them like criminals and take them in, they delivered them to Bellevue, which, because it was a city hospital, could turn no one away. Mark and I met often. Even though he once grabbed me by the neck (which taught me to always sit by the door during our therapy sessions), we got along quite well. In fact, once we were playing basketball and, after jumping up, he came down hard on me before I could step away. He was terribly sorry, and for days thereafter inquired if I was okay. We allied in a new way after that incident.

One day, when I was in seminar, there was an urgent knock on the door: "Dean, you've got to come to the ward! Mark's been put in a camisole [straitjacket], and is completely disoriented. He's in the padded room."

I excused myself and rushed to the ward. I found Mark sitting in the corner of the darkened room. He seemed terrified. He looked up at me, and just kept repeating my name. I tried to calm him, and said I would return immediately. I ran to the nurses' station and grabbed his chart. It seemed that at lunchtime, he had been causing a disturbance, threatening another patient. The nurses called a psychiatric resident (who did not "reside" on the ward and always needed to be called). That doctor prescribed the antipsychotic Haldol by mouth. Now, Haldol is a very powerful psychotropic drug, which is regrettably often used more for ward management than treatment.

Also, such a drug, given orally, takes some time to take effect. About half an hour later, there was a nursing shift. Mark was acting up again, threatening a patient with a chair. Without looking at the chart, the nurse called for a resident. A different resident arrived and—again, without consulting the chart—ordered Haldol by injection. Mark was given this second dose and went into something of a cataleptic state.

I got Mark strapped into a wheelchair and rushed him through the underground tunnel over to the Bellevue Hospital Children's Emergency Room. I went to the desk and explained the situation; a nurse said a resident would be right with me. I returned to Mark and sat down next to him, holding his hand and talking quietly to him. A resident appeared, holding a hypodermic syringe in the air, and approached a young child sitting on his mother's lap. Upon seeing the needle, the child screamed. Then every child in the emergency room started screaming. The shot was given.

I bolted out of my chair and confronted the resident: "Come with me." I took him into a corridor and read him the riot act. "What you have just done is terrorize a group of children and their parents. You have also violated the patient's privacy by administering treatment publicly. All of this was unnecessary and unethical."

The resident kept staring at my identification, which was clipped to my pocket. Because of my new position, it read DEAN WILLIAM RUDOY, FACULTY. I realized that this young doctor most likely thought I was an academic dean. Good: rather than disabuse him of his assumption, I used it.

"You are never to conduct yourself that way again."

"Yes, sir."

I returned to Mark. At last, a resident appeared and took us into a small room, where, after hearing the story of the Haldol overdose, he administered an intravenous drug into a vein in the back of Mark's hand. Within minutes, Mark came out of his cataleptic state, fully aware of himself, me, and his surroundings. I wheeled him back to the ward; he was now relatively calm and collected.

I am sure that it has escaped neither your attention, nor your sense of irony, that this boy was at a psychiatric hospital being treated for drug abuse ("popping" cocaine into the veins in the back of his hand)—and now the medical establishment had overdosed him and, most fortunately, brought him back with yet another drug.

Eventually, Mark was discharged into the care of an aunt; but Bellevue was ready for his eventual return, as was the case with so many Bellevue Kids.

*

My years at Bellevue were filled with such stories, all of which penetrated my academic studies and defensive shields. Nothing could have prepared me for the experience. I came through it all transformed as a therapist, and as a man.

His Smile Comes Back to Me

Three months after my psychology internship ended at Bellevue Hospital, I received a phone call one evening from Sam, the chief psychologist on the adolescent ward. Bobby had committed suicide. The staff got together and asked if I would return to deliver the eulogy.

I had not been Bobby's therapist, but—as with all the kids—I knew him pretty well. He was a kind and compassionate boy. Of course I would speak at the funeral.

A child's death, particularly by his own hand, is out of the natural order of things. What can one say in such a eulogy? I went up to the roof of my apartment building and stood there, staring at the sky. A cool, quiet breeze drifted through the city across the tops of the buildings. I took a candle from my pocket and lit it, then cupped my hands around the flame to keep it safe.

His smile comes back to me.

When I first met Bobby, he smiled. He didn't save up his smiles. He gave them away, generously. His was dazzling, the kind that lights up both the face of the one who wears it and the one who receives it. Yet sometimes that smile faltered, like a candle's flame unsettled by the wind. Then, behind the brightness, one could glimpse the shadows of his unbearable sadness.

I remember seeing him sitting with other children on the ward, comforting them as they cried in their private unhappiness. He would place his arm around them, lean into them, and speak softly, soothingly. I never heard what it was he said to them.

We who knew Bobby, we who were moved by his story, touched by his presence, wanted to protect that flame: to nourish it, to surround it with our hands, to block the cold wind, to keep it safe. And yet, a child such as Bobby, who has no family, whose impoverished environment is empty of warmth and encouragement, is faced with a life task of almost insurmountable difficulty, if he is to survive: *to adopt himself*, lovingly. We who have chosen to dedicate ourselves to the well-being of these children can hold them in care, comfort them, work with them, so that they can begin to care for and about themselves. But we cannot keep them entirely safe. The cold winds of their own despair, the life-denying environments from which they come and to which they return, can too easily extinguish the flame of their vulnerable youth.

The day of Bobby's funeral brought some broader issues to human scale: the corrosive conditions concealed within a society of wealth and luxury—poverty, ignorance, callous neglect, conditions that rob people of hope, and children of a future.

We may effect a change in the *content* of a child's life, but without a commensurate change in the *context* within which he lives, any gain can only be temporary. We watch this happen and are, therefore, obliged to extend our vision beyond the horizon of what we see: to do what we can to correct, beyond the isolated wards and corridors of hospitals, the social conditions that hurt children.

On the day of the funeral, I joined other members of the ward staff—a doctor, a few nurses, social workers, and activity therapists—at a small church near the hospital. There I delivered my thoughts and memories about Bobby to them, and to a couple of Bobby's distant relatives. We took him in his casket, donated by a charity, to Potter's Field in the Bronx, a cemetery for the impoverished, and quietly buried him along with several gifts from the kids on the ward: a marijuana joint, coins, a dollar bill.

I like to think that once Bobby moved out of form, he slipped through a portal to a peaceful place where he has no memory of the private sufferings that haunted him. I suppose that is all we can do: create in our imaginations a place of comfort for those who have left us behind, while we collect and save the pieces of our broken hearts.

The Door

Every child has a birthright: to experience delight and joy; health and well-being; safety and security; to unfold to their fullest promise by being nourished in body, mind, and spirit; to be loved; and to live in peace. In far too many instances, children are not given these things.

In the late 1980s, I worked as a counselor at a youth center in New York City called The Door. It was a remarkable place, offering comprehensive health, family planning, educational, arts, vocational, and therapeutic services to any kid who walked across the threshold. Many of these young people were living on the street, having run away or been thrown away, but the population crossed the entire socioeconomic spectrum.

I remember my job interview. I had given a lot of thought to what I was going to wear, and left my apartment dressed in pressed khaki slacks, ironed shirt, and tie. When I arrived at the center, I discovered the staff in t-shirts and jeans, and got the impression that most of them played the role of 'friend' toward the kids. This presented me with something of a challenge: my choice of clothing was meant not only to show respect for the professional work for which I hoped to be hired, but also to present the kids with an image of an adult who, although perhaps a bit conventional and buttoned-down, was fully available to them. Besides which, I wasn't there to be their friend; I was there to be their counselor. I was hired.

*

One of my kids was David. He had had cerebral palsy from birth, and was able to walk with what he called his "sticks": two metal crutches. One day, as he arrived, he slipped and fell. I rushed over to help.

"No thanks, Dean. My foster mom says you don't drown by falling into a puddle. You drown by not getting up." And then, with extraordinary effort, he rose.

David was a gallant young man, and quite poetic. He used a certain expression when describing the start of anything new: "from the giddy-up." I adopted that from him, and have used it pretty much every day since. Whenever I say it, I think of him with great fondness and respect.

*

Ricardo was a slight, gentle, bespectacled boy. Having experienced quite a bit of bullying within his macho culture, he had built up a store of anger within himself. In fact, when he spoke of the altercations he'd been in—some of which he had instigated himself—he often expressed his anger at his "habit of fighting" by hitting himself on the legs with his fists:

"Why do I keep making the same mistakes over and over!"

"First of all, please stop hitting yourself. Look, you've made mistakes. If any of us tried to walk a straight line, we would list a little to the right and a little to the left. It's the way we're made. I see your struggle. You don't want to be passive. You don't want to be aggressive. What's the middle way?"

"Maybe being calm."

"Okay, that's now your path. Try to visualize it."

We worked on creating, in his imagination, a new image of himself walking with ease, dignity, and self-respect. This was to become his new habit, which would take a lot of practice before it took hold. In the meantime, he would fall or be pushed off that path, then need to forgive himself and get back on it.

We had worked together for months when he told me he wanted to become a doctor. Several sessions later, he arrived with a black eye and bruised hands, reporting that he had been in a fight. Because of the noise in the youth center (which was formerly a department store and was now just a huge, open space divided by modular walls), counseling took place with chairs very close together. I reached toward him urgently, and carefully held his hands in mine.

"If these are to be the hands of a healer, you have an obligation to take care of them." I don't think any adult in Ricardo's life had ever touched him in that way, with that degree of concern. His eyes filled with tears.

"Okay, Dean. I will."

*

Ahmed arrived at The Door and registered. At his initial entry interview, during which he was introduced to all of the services available, it was suggested that he sign up for counseling. He made an appointment, and I was assigned to him. During our first session, he sat down and stared at me with contempt.

"Are you a Jew?"

I had learned in both my education and training that the therapist is in charge of the boundaries within the therapeutic relationship, but while we might be aware of those perimeters, many patients are not. Sometimes very direct, personal questions will be presented to us. For example, I once worked with a parent who complained about her son's lack of responsibility, and asked, "Do you have kids?"

Of course, this is a reasonable question that most people in everyday exchanges would answer directly. However, in a therapeutic conversation, it is fruitful to discover what motivates the question, to listen with the "third ear." And so, I replied: "That is an important question that I would be happy to answer a little later. But first, can we talk a bit about why that question arises now?"

"Well, I figured if *you* have kids, they're probably perfect. You know just how to handle them."

You see what happened there? The patient assumed, because I was a therapist, that I must be a flawless parent. That assumption would have had an impact, and could have blocked whatever empathic connection and understanding we were developing.

"Well, because I'm a psychologist doesn't mean that I'm automatically a perfect parent. And if I'm a parent, that doesn't make me an expert at being one. Maybe you're wondering if I'm really going to be able to understand your situation and help you."

"Yes. I guess that's it."

"Well, my education, training, and experience have prepared me to help you, and I believe I can. But of course, you will be the judge of that." By that time, the original question really no longer needed to be answered, because the true concern underlying it had been addressed.

Back to Ahmed.

"That's a significant question, and I will answer it in just a bit," I said. "But first, please tell me why it's important to you."

"There's no way I'm meeting with a Jew."

"Well, then, out of respect for both of us, I will refer you to someone else."

Sometimes, the patient draws the boundary.

*

Once, a young man arrived for his first appointment with me. He sat down, sprawled across the chair, and shoved a piece of paper toward me.

"You gotta sign this."

I had learned that many of the kids at the center had problems reading, so, lest I embarrass him, I did not ask directly whether or not he had read the paper: "Do you know what this says?"

"Yeah. The court says you gotta sign it."

I read the document. "You've been remanded for counseling by the court, and are required to attend a dozen sessions. If we decide to work together, I'll be happy to sign this after we meet twelve times." He scowled at me and crossed his arms. Several minutes went by in silence. "Is there anything you'd like to talk about?"

"No."

"You know, some kids come here wanting to talk about stuff in their lives, and find counseling to be helpful. Who knows? It could happen with us."

Silence. At the end of our session, during which only a few words were spoken, we made our next appointment. He showed up the next week, mostly because he had to; but he began to talk about his life. By the twelfth session, we had actually done some good work, and decided to continue.

*

One day I was walking through what we called "Center Space." There were tables and chairs there, where kids could just hang out. A young mother, about fifteen years old, was there with her baby in a stroller.

The baby was fussing and crying loudly. Other kids began yelling at her to "shut that kid up or leave." I saw her tense up and raise her arm. She was going to strike the child. By that time, from behind, I had reached her. I placed my hands on her shoulders and whispered, "You don't want to do that." She broke down in tears. "Let's go over there," I said.

We went over to the counseling area and talked about the stresses she was enduring. As she was not the only child-with-a-child at The Door, we had formed a young mothers' group, and I suggested it might be helpful to her. It was.

*

One of the most important lessons I learned at The Door was the limit on what I could accomplish with these kids, given the tough and often punishing circumstances of their lives. But when I walked beside them for a while, I also saw the life force in each of them, the resilience and hope. Thirty years have now passed. I often think of them, and imagine their lives fulfilled. Who knows? Sometimes the most fervent prayers are answered.

The White Painting

The Museum of Modern Art was a place of refuge and restoration for me on many an afternoon, while I was living in New York. I was particularly drawn to the art of the Abstract Expressionists and color field painters such as Mark Rothko, Helen Frankenthaler, Hans Hoffman, and Barnett Newman. I felt more engaged by these paintings than those that were objective or figurative, which, though impressive in their virtuosity, did not invite me to participate. The colors of the Abstract Expressionist paintings, and the vibrating edges where the colors met, drew me in.

One afternoon, while walking through the museum, I entered an empty gallery and came upon a large work by Newman, about six feet tall and ten feet long. At first glance, it appeared quite simply to be a blank white canvas. I stood there and soon discovered that there were, in fact, two distinct, large, white color fields of different widths and tones separated—or rather joined—by a narrow, somewhat darker white band. Several minutes passed as I first studied and then began to experience the painting.

I heard them before I saw them: half a dozen high school students burst into the room, notebooks in hand. Clearly, they were on assignment. They were making comments to each other, disparaging the paintings, making fun of that which they did not understand. They knew these were important works of art, or they would not be hanging in the museum, but they had not been prepared by their teacher to understand and accept their meanings, or how they unfolded out of the centuries of the history of painting. Quite honestly, I wanted them to go away. Eventually, they did.

I returned my attention to the white painting. About five minutes passed before I caught sight peripherally of one of the students re-entering the gallery. He wandered aimlessly from one painting to another, and eventually, and rather courageously, approached me from the side.

"Excuse me, sir, can I ask you a question?"

"Sure."

"What are you looking at?"

As a teacher, I felt the impulse to give this fellow a lecture about the virtues of Abstract Expressionist art, and to tell him exactly what I saw and what I was experiencing. Surprisingly, however, I restrained myself.

"Have you got a few minutes?"

"Yeah."

"Okay, let's just stand here, and you tell me what you see."

"Well, I see a white painting."

"Okay, that's a good start. Let's watch it." A couple of minutes passed.

"Wait a minute! Something's moving."

"What do you see?"

"It's like shadows on a wall, and they're moving."

"What could that be?"

"Well, it's like there's a tree behind us, and the sun behind *that*, and there's a breeze and the leaves are moving."

"Where are we?"

"It's like in the Greek islands, where they have all those white houses."

The painting had taken on life. We continued talking about what he was seeing, which included a door ajar (where that narrow white band appeared). And we talked about what he imagined: a family that lived in the house, and a lazy dog lying beside us in a patch of sun, and birds in the trees.

Ending our visit, he said he had to go. "Thanks a lot. This was fun."

I like to think that this young man will always now see paintings with more than his eyes, and allow his imagination to participate in the experience.

As has often been said, "That which is learned with pleasure is learned full measure."

And so it was.

Bending the Rules

When I started out as a psychotherapist, while still in graduate school, I guided my conduct by a set of rather rigid rules. I convinced myself that these guidelines were meant to protect my patients. In fact, they were employed mostly to defend myself.

One of my rules was that I would never be the first to speak in session, as I wanted to respect the right of the patient to bring up whatever they wanted to discuss. This particular injunction was put to the test one afternoon, when a relatively new patient arrived for his appointment.

When this young man had first come to see me, the presenting problem was his vocational ambivalence. The son and grandson of Christian ministers, he also had chosen to be 'of the cloth.' Or had he *been* chosen? For several weeks, that was the terrain of our explorations.

Another of my rules was that I would never touch a patient. There are good psychotherapeutic reasons for this proscription. While our intention when we touch another person may very well be benign, that touch may not be received as such—especially if the patient has a complicated history of physical encounters. Our touch might be interpreted as intrusive, or even seductive. I modified my rule for this particular patient, as he always began and ended our sessions with a handshake. As long as he initiated, I felt it was okay to reciprocate, as refusing someone's hand is quite simply rude.

We were into the third month of our work when he arrived, closed the door behind him, and, as always, approached me with his hand outstretched. We silently shook, and took our seats. He smiled at me; I smiled back and nodded. A minute or two passed in silence, during which he either looked at the floor or at the ceiling or at me. Although, non-verbally, I extended an invitation for him to speak, he did not.

After about five minutes, I began to question my rule about not initiating conversation. Ten minutes ... Twenty. We settled in, both now actually somewhat comfortable in the silence. Occasionally our eyes would meet, to check in with one another. The entire fifty-minute session went by in silence. He then stood, as did I. He approached me, hand outstretched. We shook. "Thank you," he said. And he departed.

When I met with my supervisor later that day, I said: "I don't have anything to report. My patient didn't say a word during our session. Nothing happened."

"Don't be so sure."

The following week, my patient arrived. We shook hands and he took his seat. He smiled. I smiled and nodded. A couple of minutes went by in silence, and I settled into my chair, expecting a repeat experience.

"I'd like to tell you why I really came into therapy." I hope that my sudden alarm at this statement did not show in my face. *What was I about to hear? What terrible secret was this man about to reveal to me?* I nodded. "I sometimes go to peep shows and watch," he continued.

Whew! No big deal. No big deal to *me*, but enormous to him, given his position in the community. He was wracked with guilt and shame. I remained calm and available to hear his 'confession.' At the end of the session, he said: "Even though I didn't say anything last time, a lot happened. I felt comfortable just sitting here with you. You didn't push or pull. I felt accepted. And I trusted you. That's why I can talk about these things now."

Over the next several months, we spent the rest of our time together exploring these issues, which, in fact, were related to his original presenting problem—his admission ticket into therapy. Did he really want to be a minister? Did he feel a familial obligation to pursue a profession that had been handed down to him by his father and grandfather? We also addressed his sexual identity, his romantic attractions and erotic desires. What began as therapy that could be considered vocational counseling evolved into a far deeper examination of this man's internal life.

Although we might like to think that different aspects of ourselves reside in separate rooms in the mansions of our minds, the doors to those rooms are often open, and those characteristics—those characters—speak with one another.

In our last session, this man thanked me for "walking beside" him as he addressed significant questions about his private and public identities. He was prepared to continue exploring these matters on his own. He was confident that he would eventually reach a favorable resolution.

He rose and approached me. I offered my hand, and we shook.

*

Many years later, now in private practice and less preoccupied with self-protective rules, I was working with a young man who had been diagnosed with depression. He spoke little, and found it difficult to make eye contact. One day, in the middle of a rather unproductive therapy session, I asked, "Would you like to take a walk outside?"

"Are we allowed?"

"I don't see why not."

We put on our jackets and left the office. Once outside, walking side by side under the autumn trees, away from the pressure of a face-to-face encounter, he began to open up. Most of our sessions from that point forward were held outside, walking and talking. Trust grew under those trees. It was during one of those walks that he told me, "You'll probably think I'm crazy, but I heard a voice once, out of nowhere."

"First of all, I don't think you're crazy. And as far as hearing things that other people don't hear, well, that doesn't make your experience any less real or meaningful."

"It was just two words."

"Oh?"

"God grows."

On that brisk, new, sunlit day, out under the endless blue sky, who could have argued with the truth of that declaration?

To Memorize You

When she arrived for our session, she was angry at me. This was not unusual. It was either something I said or didn't say last week, and I was now to pay. As disconcerting as it was to be verbally assaulted at the commencement of a therapy session, I had grown accustomed to it over the past couple of years. In any case, after the initial pent-up barrage, we got down to work. She told me that, as a child, she was considered a gifted sculptor.

"Have you continued making art?"

"No. And it's too late. I've lost all the opportunities and development I could have had over all those years."

"Do you miss it?"

"Of course I do! What an ignorant question."

Several days later, I dropped by an art supply shop in the city and saw something that brought our conversation to mind. The following week, when she arrived, I told her about it.

"Over at the art supply store on Carlisle Street, they have some red clay. I thought you might like to get some. Don't make anything with it. Just knead it. Rub it into your skin and under your fingernails. Smell it. Taste it."

"That's a ridiculous idea."

I smiled.

The following week, she arrived in a temper, carrying a box. On the very top was an oilcloth, which she threw open and lay on the carpet.

"Get out of your chair and sit on the floor!"

I followed her instruction. She reached into the box and opened a plastic bag, grabbed a chunk of clay, and threw it at me. I caught it. She also took a chunk. We spent the hour kneading the clay and talking as if it wasn't even there.

"I want to sculpt you."

"Why?"

"I want to memorize you."

We agreed that she could bring a stand with clay, which I would place in the corner of my office, covered with a wet towel to keep the clay moist and the bust private.

Over the ensuing weeks, we continued our therapeutic work, talking about her painful childhood and its repercussions into adulthood. She told me that now, when she dreamed of those early years, I was there. I could do nothing, but my presence was a comfort. All the while, she modeled the bust.

"I know when therapy will end."

"Oh?"

"When I've completed the bust." After a couple more months, she said: "I need one more session, and I'll be done. After that, would you be willing to come to my home one time? I want to show you the sculptures I've been making."

"Yes. I would like that."

The following week, she put the finishing touches on the bust. We loaded it into her truck and she drove me to her home. Her work was astonishingly beautiful: small, perfectly proportioned figures.

"I want you to have one; any one you like."

I selected a piece, thanked her, and she walked me to the door. We looked at one another for a while, wished each other well, and said goodbye.

She had memorized me. And I shall not forget her.

As If It Were Yesterday

"Again! Again!" she insisted.

"But aren't you tired?" I pleaded.

"Again! Again!"

Little Jessie, my three-year-old friend, wanted to be swung and spun over and over again in the tire hanging from the big oak tree in her backyard. Her delight in the repetition was no surprise to me. She enjoyed everything that repeated: the *tick-tock* of my pocket watch, the singsong of her nursery rhymes, the *101 Dalmatians* read at least that many times.

Who knows why kids like repetition? Some psychologists say they are trying to master their experience, such as when a child finishes a fairy tale (heard for the umpteenth time) right along with you, or when they can finally pick up all the jacks after a million tries. Repetition is also comforting—the rocking in the cradle, the humming of a well-worn tune. Ever see a child in a reverie staring into space, thumb in mouth, fingers twirling hair? All these examples of repetitive behavior are normal and healthy. The child eventually *grows out of it*.

*

"Again! Again!" he complained. "I can't believe I did it again!"

My patient Jack had recently had an argument with his supervisor, which nearly lost him his job. It seems this had happened before, at other work sites: "Dammit! I should have seen this coming. I've got a temper, and he knows just how to push my buttons, just like my dad."

Why do some people keep repeating the same mistakes over and over again? Some psychologists say this "repetition compulsion" is the product of unfinished business from long ago. The person repeats old patterns in the vain hope of coming up with a different ending. Others say it's old, learned behavior that doesn't change with new experience, because the person's way of thinking, feeling, and behaving have become inflexible. Though certainly not uncommon, these examples of repetitive behavior are abnormal and unhealthy. These people have *grown into it.*

After over thirty-five years in the field of psychology, I've drawn the conclusion that all kinds of human behavior—from the usual to the most unusual—are related to one another. They lie along a continuum. Take repetition, for example. The two stories above reflect two ends of a continuum: healthy repetition (rhythmic games, songs, stories, and rituals of childhood that are pitched toward growth and *tomorrow*) and unhealthy repetition (rigid communication habits and destructive relationship patterns of adulthood that are pitched toward stagnation and *yesterday*).

As it turned out, my patient Jack was "living today as if it were yesterday," repeating old, defiant habits and patterns that continued to cause him discomfort and despair. He was spinning his wheels. He wanted to change, but he didn't know how. He asked me what psychotherapy was all about.

"It's all about today, as well as recognizing the power of the past, in which we all learned ways of being that may not serve us well. It's only here and now, today, where we can find fertile ground for change and growth and freedom."

"How do I get free?"

"Well, I'd suggest a journey in three parts. Let's talk about hindsight, insight, and foresight. You certainly have 20/20 hindsight. You know you have a temper. You know you have buttons. And you know it's gotten you into trouble several times."

"Yeah, but why do I always overreact?"

"Well, actually, I don't think there *is* any such thing as an overreaction. Our emotional response to something might seem out of proportion to a particular circumstance; however, if we open the frame, we will see other things that might explain it. You've already identified something important, someone standing just offstage."

"You mean my dad."

"Yes. And you see, we are already on Part Two of the journey."

Over several sessions, we explored Jack's stormy relationship with his father, who had been harshly critical of him while he was growing up and often humiliated him in front of others.

"All of us look at life through spectacles. The prescription was set in childhood. When you look at your supervisors through those lenses, you assume they are judging you as your father did, when in fact they might just be trying to get the work done. Old emotions rise, and you get caught up in an attitude of defiance. When push comes to shove, they win and you lose, once again feeling powerless and humiliated just like when you were a kid."

"It happens so fast."

"Yes. Those old spectacles we all wear sometimes cause us to misperceive our present circumstances. Actually, it's the way our brains work. We're given a little bit of information, and the brain fills in the rest of the picture from our past experiences. It's efficient, but often unreliable. As for the speed, I have a suggestion. Touch your right index finger with your thumb like this. This will now be your pause button. When you become aware of the old feelings arising, press that button before reacting. Give yourself a momentary time-out to reflect."

"Foresight."

"Yes."

Over time, we went deeper into Jack's emotional life. He identified anger as his most familiar feeling. However, if anger is the fire, what's the fuel?

"Although anger is a very dramatic emotion," I said, "and gets a lot of attention, and appears to be a direct response to a particular event, I believe that when we feel it we are angry not so much about the *event*, but about another unspoken feeling we are having."

"I don't follow."

"You've told me that the way your father treated you as a boy made you angry. Might there have been another feeling, just before the anger?"

Jack fell silent and stared at the carpet. We sat there quietly.

Later in our work, Jack brought in a dream. As he related it, another dream of his came to my mind, and I was excited to link the two together. Therapists have egos, too, of course: not only would this linkage be useful to him, but I could show off my intuitive acumen. So while he was talking of one thing, I was thinking of another, making my plan.

When he finished, I said, "You know, this dream reminds me of another you told me some time ago, and I think putting them together might be helpful." As I reminded him of his previous dream, a look of confusion crossed his face. I chose to ignore it, and waxed on.

When I finished: "That wasn't my dream."

I sort of wish I could have seen my face at that moment. He was right. The second dream was from another patient. What was I to do? How could I get out of this jam? After a long silence, during which I failed to come up with a strategy to save face, I offered: "I am so sorry. You're right. That second dream was from another patient. I have failed you in this moment."

He looked at me for a long time, and then dropped his gaze to the floor. "My father never apologized to me." And in that moment, in which a therapeutic error had been made, reparation began.

Our work from that time forward addressed Jack's grief. There was an empty place in his heart where a father's love and acceptance should have resided. He came to understand that. He also came to understand that his father's own childhood had been similar to his, and that, although his father never awakened to it, Jack was now committed to doing so—and as a result, he might not only heal himself, but his father as well.

I'm Not Sad

Most of our first therapy session was taken up with the young woman's tears. She asked if she might take a tissue from the box that sat on the table next to her.

"Of course."

During the entire session, although she cried many times, she never took a second tissue. She simply folded the one she had, over and over again. That spoke volumes. As the months went by, it became abundantly clear that this young woman felt unworthy of even the slightest bit of kindness or consideration. When I had earned her trust, we spoke of that, and how self-abasement played out in both her personal and work lives. She chose cruel and callous men for partners, and found it impossible to speak up for herself to her imperious boss.

"I'm just a worn-out, gray doormat, I guess."

As a result of a traumatic upbringing, she had internalized the contempt of her family and was convinced of her unworthiness. She behaved in such a way, and made life choices, so as to repeat the script she had been given, which she knew by heart. She knew no other way.

And … yet. She had had the extraordinary courage to enter psychotherapy. Each time she crossed the threshold to my office was a challenge. However, something within her—perhaps her own voice, which she had never heard—compelled her to continue.

I have taught my students: "Whatever your patient presents, consider that the opposite might equally be true." This patient thought very little of herself. But behind that mask of self-contempt, so carefully constructed by early influences and shaped by later events, was a person yearning to be seen and heard, to be understood and touched with kindness.

As with many women in our culture in a similar place, she was somewhat detached from her body and its wisdom. We often spoke about situations in which she found herself, when her body signaled danger but her mind rejected its warnings. Slowly, in our work, she started to listen more carefully to herself.

One day, I said something to her that hit home: "We cannot *be* what we possess, or what we think, or what we feel, whether that is a thing or a thought or an emotion. Who we *are* resides behind all the phenomena of this life, watching." She began to witness her life, not just live it.

She also learned that she had a right to act and speak on her own behalf. During one session, she told me that an uncle had died. Although she was estranged from her family, she wanted to pay her respects: "But I'm afraid when I go there, my aunt is going to attack me. I guess I can just sit in a corner."

"Well, that's one strategy. Here's another: when you enter the funeral parlor, find your aunt. Approach her immediately. Extend your hand and offer your condolences. Then, go sit in the corner."

We rehearsed it over and over again, until she was comfortable. When she arrived for our session following the funeral, she entered the room in a new way. Her demeanor was different; confident. She had taken charge of a difficult situation rather than letting that situation govern her.

We rehearsed other scenarios, populated with people in her personal and work lives. She began to speak with a self-assured voice she had never known she possessed. One day, during a session, she began to cry. Still reticent to take a tissue, she hesitated, and only did so when I nodded. I leaned forward and asked her: "What are the tears saying?"

"Oh, I'm not sad. I'm just full of emotion."

Several weeks later, I was relating to her a story of my work with street kids in New York City, a particular experience that was relevant to the subject of our conversation in that moment. I began to cry. She looked at me with great concern.

"Don't worry," I said. "I'm not sad. I'm just full of emotion." And we laughed.

We continued to work together for several years. During our last session, she boldly told me: "I don't know if I will remember all that you have taught me, all of your words. But I will always remember the way you treated me." She then reached into her bag, took out a small painting she had made, and handed it to me. "This says what I can't."

It was a beautiful explosion of color, which still hangs on my wall.

Farewell, My Patients

When it came time for me to close my private practice, I told all my patients about six months beforehand, so that we all might come in for a smooth landing. Ambivalence on both sides was inevitable upon approaching the termination of our work together. Pairing affects the partners. Neither they nor I wanted to experience the loss, but I knew from the beginning that within our very first *hello* was an implied *goodbye*. Central to therapeutic work is the fostering of the patient's independence, which should be celebrated at each step in the process, including the crossing of the threshold back out into the world—without me.

We are not very good, in this culture, at saying goodbye, even though it occurs as frequently as hello. Many endings are abrupt and wrenching and break the heart, or are long and drawn-out and shred it to pieces, or are unacknowledged and mourned privately, unresolved.

I knew these things. The termination of a therapeutic relationship should be different, and provide a model for future goodbyes in the patient's life, in that time is taken to examine and understand the emotions and thoughts that accompany the parting. The parting should be clean, and the end should be clear; however, it must be handled with a certain finesse. The therapist must never abandon a patient.

I knew that some of my patients would need to borrow some of my confidence in their capacity to make it on their own. But that would be nothing new, as I knew they had borrowed the same confidence along the arduous path of the therapy itself. The fact is, the therapy would go on and the insights would continue to arise even in my absence, as my patients had internalized both me and our conversations in memory—both would continue to inform their lives as time goes by.

Bottom line: there comes a time for the chick to break out of the egg, for the butterfly to struggle from the confines of the cocoon. That necessary process of birth can be frightening, but I was committed to being there for each of my patients as an encouraging midwife, and, once the birth had taken place, to wish the hatchlings well … and to retreat.

I knew that closing my practice was unlike the organic termination of therapy, to which both any patient and I might mutually agree. This ending was unilateral. In the former instance, which I had experienced with various patients, I made clear that I would remain available to them for any 'tune-ups' they might seek or require. This was different. For all my patients, I provided a list of three therapists to whom they might go following our work, if they wished to continue with therapy. However, in most cases, I suggested that they wait several months—both to give themselves a chance to experience our goodbye, and to try out their wings on their own. I also knew that if they entered another therapy immediately after ours, they would impose the expectations born of our work onto the new therapist, which would interfere with that new bonding.

Some of my patients, learning of my decision to close the practice, inquired whether or not there could be any post-therapy contact. In some instances, this question arose out of anxiety, fear of not being able to make it without me. For some, it was the consequence of sadness at the loss of someone of whom they had become fond. For others, it was a wish to now become friends. I knew all this to be true for them, because I, too, had some of these feelings.

This brought to mind the memory of a former student's experience. He had worked with a patient for several months, very much enjoying the sessions, as the patient and he shared many of the same interests. When the therapy ended, the patient suggested they remain in contact and have lunch sometime. The therapist agreed. When they met for a meal, the former patient asked the therapist some personal questions, and the therapist eagerly answered, free at last from professional constraints and now able to reveal himself to the former patient.

As the therapist waxed about his own life, he noticed that the former patient became quite uncomfortable. They talked about it a bit. As it turned out, the patient had a fantasy image of the therapist, developed over the time of their work together, which was now being threatened by the latter's personal revelations. In addition, the mutuality of a personal conversation was by its very nature transgressing the hierarchical structure of the therapeutic relationship that had been established over time. The lunch did not go well, and they agreed that it would not be a good idea to pursue further contact. My former student showed a great deal of courage in relating this story to me, and closed by saying: "You were right. A clean ending would have been better for both of us."

Having experienced the privilege of working with these brave people, of earning their trust, of witnessing their growth, and knowing we would not see one another again, made saying goodbye a difficult task. Each had become dear to me, and I felt the loss. But the knowledge that, along the way, they had discovered within themselves resources of hope and confidence to sustain them in facing challenges up ahead, has at least softened the finale and sufficed to comfort me, when I miss them.

Fare well, my patients.

BIG SKY / LONG HORIZON

"I didn't take the dirt. I didn't need to."

Collecting Some Dirt

There is, in northern New Mexico, a little town called Chimayó, a Spanish village at the center of which is an old church. Inside the church there is a little room with a hole in the floor. The dirt inside the hole is said to have healing properties.

In my kitchen, I opened a drawer and plucked out a small, plastic sandwich bag; I was on my way to Chimayó.

After a couple of hours' drive, I arrived in the parking lot of the church. As soon as I opened the car door, I felt the hot, dry summer sun beating down on me. I walked to the church and stepped across the threshold into the dark, cool, timeless space of sanctuary.

I was alone. When my eyes adjusted, I walked to the back of the church toward the room. First there was a little anteroom with canes and crutches hanging on the walls, evidence of miracles that had occurred there. I walked through another doorway, into the inner chamber. Standing in the hole was an elderly woman; a small boy rubbed dirt on her legs. I turned quietly and walked back into the adjoining room to wait. Eventually, they came out. We nodded silently at one another, and they left.

I walked back into the chamber and approached the hole, reaching into my pocket for the plastic bag. I stooped down to scoop up some of the dirt. But I stopped. I couldn't do it. This made no sense to me; since boyhood, I have collected stones and rocks and dirt from all sorts of places, and I knew that people took dirt from the church all the time (and that the priest regularly refilled the hole with dirt from out back). And, yet.

I slowly stood up, put the bag back in my pocket, and left the room. As I walked through the sanctuary, I tried to figure out what had just happened. Outside the church is a little stream. I sat down on a warm rock and watched the water flow, glistening in the sun.

From my childhood memories wafted up a little phrase I had learned by heart decades earlier: *The whole Earth is full of glory.* As I sat there, that phrase began to make sense. If the dirt is holy, then the sides of the hole that contain the dirt are also holy … and the floor in which the hole resides is holy … and the ground upon which the floor rests … and the stone on which I sat … and the stream … and even I am holy, and so on and on. The hole of holiness—the whole of holiness—has no perimeter.

I didn't take the dirt. I didn't need to.

It's in Here

When I first met her, she was sitting in the corner of an art gallery belonging to a friend of mine, quietly beading a bag. She looked up and smiled at me when we were introduced. I knew then that we were to be friends.

Mary Attu of the Aleut tribe earned her living making beautiful medicine bags of soft, smoked, brain-tanned deer hide the traditional way. She was a master in beadwork, having won many awards; her work was represented in several museums, including the Smithsonian. She also built props for Kevin Costner's movie *Dances with Wolves*, and liked to tell the story of when she asked him what he wanted her to fill the pillows with for a particular tepee scene. ("What would they have been filled with?" "Buffalo fur." "Well, then, buffalo fur.")

Upon learning that I did not own a medicine bag, she made one for me, beaded on the front with the traditional Aleut "drop of water" diamond design, and placed within it important medicine: a piece of turquoise, a piece of white shell, and some sage. I wore that medicine bag every day, hung from the belt loop of my jeans, and added to its contents along the way. I took it with me as I traveled as far away as the Atlantic and Pacific Oceans, where I lay it on the sand under the sun.

As our friendship developed over time, I would visit Mary in her apartment in Albuquerque. She always had the bags she had recently made laid out on the bed. We would look at them and talk about them, and I would buy several to give to friends. For every bag she sold, she gave one away. The fact that she owned very little in material possessions, and that the income from the bags was quite modest, made her generosity all the more remarkable.

"Great Spirit will provide all that I need—no more, no less."

I remember bringing some friends who were visiting from New York City over to her place. They had all heard about Mary from me, and each had a medicine bag that I had given to them. They were eager to meet her. We arrived at her small apartment and, after introductions, looked at her most recent creations. As decisions were being made about which bags were going to be bought, my friend Helen saw a pair of Mary's turquoise earrings on her dresser.

"These are beautiful."

Mary went over, picked up the earrings, and placed them into Helen's hand, which she then covered with her own. Looking directly at her, she said: "These belong to you."

One had to learn to be careful admiring anything of Mary's, lest you leave with more than you came for.

One time I was looking over her new bags, and was drawn to one in particular. As I pointed to it, tears began to run down my cheeks. To this day, I have no idea why.

She placed it in my hand, and said: "This is your bag." And so, it was.

Over the years, I bought many bags from Mary, sometimes with particular people in mind, but most often not. Once I said: "I have no idea to whom I'm going to give these bags."

"They'll go to whom they belong." She saw us all as intermediaries, passing things along.

Mary was generous not only in a material way, but also in intellect and spirit. One day, I was telling her about various regrets I have had about my life. For example, although I enjoyed practicing and teaching psychology, as a boy I had wanted to be a symphony conductor. "I'm sorry I didn't take that fork in the road so many years ago," I said.

"Major in the major and minor in the minor," she replied. That single sentence awakened in me a realization that each of us has a repertoire of skills, set by Nature, enhanced by nurture, and advanced or not by choices we make, which needs to be respected and accepted.

Though not of the Lakota Sioux tribe, she was welcomed by the Sioux to their Sun Dance every summer. She taught me about the role of the Stand-Behind during that sacred rite: a very large circle is formed in the plaza around the Sun Dance pole, and those who have chosen to dance are pierced and tethered to the pole. As the day goes on, in the searing heat, when those in the surrounding circle see that their loved one thirsts or hungers, they drink or eat on his behalf, and pray for the well-being of all the dancers. These are the Stand-Behinds.

That story aroused my imagination, and my commitment to assume that role in others' lives, for there is not a person alive who is not carrying a secret burden or making a personal sacrifice, who could not use some support.

One day, on my way to the city to take Mary out to lunch, I realized I had forgotten to wear my medicine bag. I was already halfway to town, and there wasn't time to turn around. When I got to her apartment door, I was feeling awful, as I always wanted her to see that I carried the bag with me. She opened the door and I blurted out: "I forgot to wear my bag."

She smiled quietly and reached her hand to my heart. "You needn't carry it any longer. It's in here."

Sacred Words Were Spoken

My Navajo friend Wind invited me to join her for a meal at the home of some relatives in the Cochiti Pueblo. This was an honor. I asked her what I might bring as an appropriate gift.

"Candles would be nice," she said.

We arrived in the late afternoon of a hot summer. We were eagerly welcomed, and the candles were appreciated. The modest, traditional adobe home had thick walls, which kept the house relatively warm in the winter and cool in the summer—but this day was unusually uncomfortable. There was no fan, and certainly no air conditioner. I had learned over time to leave all Anglo sensibilities at the threshold of a Native American home. There are protocols of hospitality that guide the conduct of both host and guest. Respect is the keynote sentiment.

After some friendly conversation, we sat down for the meal, and I was placed next to the father of the family. We had been talking about spiritual traditions, so before we began eating, I asked whether or not it would be all right for me to recite a Hebrew blessing over the food. The father invited me to do so. And then we settled into a fine meal.

During dinner, the room had become quite warm, and the father instructed his little daughter to open the door to let in a breeze. She got up from her chair and went to the door, which she struggled to open. I began to rise to help her, but the father placed his hand on my arm: "This is her responsibility."

After wrestling with the door for a bit, she succeeded and returned to the table, all smiles. The father thanked her.

I immediately recognized what the father had done. Had I run to the child's assistance, I would have robbed her of an opportunity to demonstrate her place of significance, of feeling the satisfaction of exerting effort in giving something to the family. I am thankful he taught me that.

Later during the meal, the father asked if I would like to hear a blessing of his people. I said I would. And then he spoke in a language I did not know, nor did I understand it. But I felt its importance, as did the family.

Later, when Wind and I were back in the car preparing to leave, she looked at me. “Do you know what happened back there?”

“Um, what do you mean?”

“Bill spoke prayers to you that no Anglo ever hears.”

And so it was that on this quiet evening, two tribes had met in a humble home in an ancient village and exchanged sacred words; our ancestors, who had waited patiently, were pleased.

The Child in the Hill

When I was a boy, I always walked with my head down. People thought I was sad. Sometimes they were right. But mostly, I was just looking for things on the ground. In fact, I was so good at finding things that, during recess, if someone lost something in the grass, they would call out, "Get Dean!" When I learned about archaeological digs, I wanted to go on one. It wasn't until about forty years later that I did.

Earthwatch, an organization that pairs university research teams with volunteers, was sponsoring a dig out in the desert in New Mexico, not far from where I live. I filled out all the necessary paperwork and was accepted for a two-week assignment. A list of equipment and suggested clothing was sent out, and I picked up everything I needed: trowel, brush, pick, broad-brimmed hat. Of course, everything was brand-new and I felt like a real rookie, but all that changed after a few days under the punishing desert sun.

We all met up at the dig site. At fifty, I was the oldest person amongst the eighteen of us. It's interesting how quickly community is formed, especially when there is a shared purpose. It's also interesting how everyone finds their place, their role in the 'family.' Because of my age, I was cast as the grandfather, the elder of the group. And because I talk a lot, I was the storyteller—sometimes of pretty funny stories, which I often related as we walked every early morning from the campsite to the dig.

Three young people in their late teens and early twenties seemed to gravitate toward me there—two young men and a young woman. They liked me, and I liked them. While I sometimes gave them counsel about their various life issues and predicaments, they shared their enthusiasm and provided a sense of meaning that comes from being asked for advice by younger people.

In the old days, archaeological digs were pretty simple and destructive affairs: a guy and a shovel searching for pots to sell. Much has changed. Great care is taken to disturb the site as little as possible. Following removal of a centimeter of dirt, measurements are made, notes written, and photographs taken. Actual digging is done only where previous—often amateur—diggers or thieves have dug and caused not only damage but destruction of historical material.

Our group was divided into three teams assigned to three separate sites on a wide expanse of land. The topography was such that we couldn't see one another, but we could holler back and forth. When anyone found something of significance—a utensil, a decorated bead, a large potsherd—they'd let out a whoop; if we weren't occupied with something of our own, we'd go running to see what was found.

One day, around noon, a sharp call came out from a nearby team. My young teammate went running, but as I was engaged in the excavation of the wall of an underground room, I remained behind. About ten minutes later, he returned, breathless: "They found a skull, a child's skull, in the side of the hill! You should see it!"

The rancher who owned the property had wanted to remove a small hill, and had brought in a bulldozer. He cut through a portion of it and, upon discovering Native American pottery artifacts, stopped and alerted the archaeological department of a nearby university: that's how our dig had begun in the first place. One of the teams was assigned to excavate the walls of the cut the rancher had made into the hill. It was in one of those walls that the discovery of the skull was made.

"No, I don't think so," I said.

"Okay, I'm going back."

I continued to work belowground on a cool wall, shaded from the heat of the sun. I put my cheek against it.

*

At the evening campfire, there was much discussion about the find. Immediately upon discovering the top of the skull, measurements and photographs were taken. The site was carefully re-covered and marked. Hypotheses were formulated: this might have been a burial mound; there might be additional remains in the hill. The decision was made not to further disturb the site. Much of the talk was academic, and, though respectful, entirely impersonal. I sat silently, staring into the fire and listening.

The following morning, we arose at dawn and headed out to our sites. As usual, a few of the horses that roamed the land quietly approached, and accompanied us along the way. One filly, with whom I had formed a kinship, walked beside me, pushing her head against my arm.

One of the members of my team looked back, "Hey, Dean, are you okay?"

"Yeah, I'm okay."

"You're pretty quiet."

At the site, I was assigned to the sifting tray. For the next hour or so, my teammates brought up buckets of dirt, which I carefully sifted, looking for artifacts. It was tedious work, and the blazing sun, even at that early hour, beat down mercilessly.

One of my young friends came up to me and asked: "Are you sure you're okay?"

"Yeah, no problems."

"But you're usually telling stories by now, or joking around with us."

"Not today, I guess."

Over the next half-hour or so, my other two young friends checked in on me. When the third, Sarah, came over and quietly touched my arm, I felt something happening. She whispered: "Dean, what's wrong?"

I caught and held my breath, and tried to control what was rising up inside. She stood quietly beside me, holding my arm, as the tears rose from somewhere deeper than I had ever felt before. Once they came, they took over. My legs gave way as I sobbed. My young friend accompanied me to the ground. Others appeared to help. She quietly brushed them away. Her act of protection moved me deeply. I didn't know what was happening to me, but I was aware of having completely lost control of myself, and of having now surrendered to feelings arising in waves, after first trying to contain them.

She helped me to my feet as I tried to stand. I took a few steps, although I couldn't see where I was going. She walked beside me. As we made our way, she held my arm, and then she said something quietly into my ear: "You are completing the grief."

We continued walking. I now saw where I was heading—to the mesa. When we first arrived days earlier, we guessed that the people who had once lived in the village on this site would have climbed to the top of this mesa to pray.

Sarah left me at the top. Over the next hour, others climbed up, one at a time, to check on me, and then departed. Eventually, when it was over, I came down on my own and walked the long walk back to the site and to the sifting tray.

Little was said. Everyone was careful. As they each came up with their bucket, I thanked them.

That night, I had a long talk with Sarah by the campfire. "What did you mean, 'You are completing the grief'?" I asked.

"It just came to me that, when this child died, the people, for some reason, couldn't stay. They buried him and left. You completed something for them, and for him."

I nodded, and stared into the fire.

The Arc

Although I was quite comfortable living in the small adobe house I had purchased in Corrales, I knew that I wanted to build my own home out in the desert someday. One autumn day, I was driving up to Santa Fe with some time to spare. I decided to turn off to see the famous Eaves Ranch, which had, on its property, a movie set where several westerns had been shot. I had also heard that there was some land for sale.

When I drove in, I found that some of the buildings were complete, while others were just façades. One of the buildings had an old wooden sign on it that said REAL ESTATE. As I got out of my car and approached it, a very tall man wearing boots and a cowboy hat came out and started walking toward me.

"Can I help you?"

"Well, I understand there might be some land out here for sale. Would you know anything about that?"

"I guess I should. I used to own it all." Mr Eaves himself. "You want me to drive you around and show you some of the lots?"

"Sure. That would be great." I got into his Cadillac, and we took off.

It has always been difficult for me to conceal my excitement when something pleases me, which, as you might expect, is an inconvenience when shopping or negotiating a deal. We visited several lots, and when we got to the last one and got out of the car, something was different. The desert stretched out before us, and the horizon was long. I felt right at home.

"You like this lot?"

"Yes."

"You wanna buy it?"

"Yes."

"You got a dollar?"

"Yes."

"Gimme a dollar."

I pulled one out of my wallet and handed it over. We shook hands.

"You just bought yourself a lot. Now, o' course, my agent's gotta get involved, and there'll be paperwork and all of that, but, as far as I'm concerned, we have a deal."

Welcome to the Wild West.

I held on to that lot for several years, and then sold it in order to buy a hill I'd found on what used to be another huge ranch. The hill, 6,400 feet above sea level, was at the edge of a nature preserve, and the views were spectacular. The fellow from whom I purchased it introduced me to an architect named Hal Dean. We met up for breakfast at a restaurant not far from the property and had the first of what were to be many animated conversations about the design of my house on the hill. I still have that first sketch, drawn out on a paper napkin.

Over a period of several months, it became clear that we shared a certain aesthetic sensibility and intention. Our dialogue began to shape our expectations of each other's individual roles in the design and construction process. Along the way, a mutual regard developed. And, like any good architect, Hal helped me when necessary to enlarge my spotlight attention to floodlight attention, in order to see the bigger picture.

Hal and I visited the site many times. We walked the topography and made note of the natural landscape patterns. We stood out under the sun, felt its heat, and watched its trajectory. We listened to the wind and charted its directions. We imagined shadows cast by structures, and we sketched by hand—a process that requires that one sees what one is looking at in order to draw it into oneself and then draw it out. We collected objects for our desks—rocks, sand, twigs—to keep us in touch with the site and its colors, textures, and scents.

It became clear to me, as I observed Hal's process, that the architect's body, informed by education, training, and experience—beyond all technology—is the key instrument of his or her work.

All our experiences on the hill were necessary activities toward the development of architectural strategies to design and build a proper, respectful container for living, to introduce into space a work of art the scale, proportions, shapes, colors, and textures of which were informed by the site. In doing so, Hal also had to take into account an inventory of my sensual preferences—visual, auditory, and tactile.

Hal invited me to describe my lifestyle, and my anticipated use of the house. He said that the design forms should be determined by the anticipated functions. I told him I wanted a sense of flow from room to room; as few walls as possible; large volumes of space; light at the center of the house radiating throughout; a blurred boundary between interior and exterior spaces; and, most importantly, that the house should appear to grow out of the site.

In our first formal meeting in his offices, I brought along a model I had built to demonstrate in three dimensions all that I wanted.

"Excuse me, Dean. Would you wait right here?"

"Sure."

After a few minutes passed, Hal returned with his entire staff, to show them what I had done.

"No client has ever built a model. This is really outstanding."

Of course, the model was only the starting point of a much deeper process, in which Hal brought to bear his own distinct and elegant vocabulary. In that process, we encountered inevitable challenges along the way. Hal always had three options ready; I still don't know out of what hat he so often pulled those.

After many months, we finally put spade to earth, and a year and a half later, I moved in.

One of the first things I noticed was rainbows. Hal had designed a stretch of windows in the stairwell. The beveled edges of the panes joined each other, creating prisms. The morning sun struck the prisms and cast rainbows into the house. He claimed not to have planned this, but I believe I know better.

Ideally, one should be as comfortable within an architectural structure as one is in one's own body—in a way, the forms should be natural extensions of our own sense of self. Hal fully accomplished this, as a result of our close and cordial collaboration.

I call my home The Arc, as it flows in that form around the hill. The radii of the arc emanate from and return to a point atop the hill, on which I first sat and asked permission to build my home there.

Hal and I became very dear friends. The greatest gift he gave me, far beyond the beauty of his design, was to extend the perimeter of his family to "the other Dean," and I have had the pleasure of knowing and loving his wife and children, and their children, for over twenty years now.

When he passed away, his wife Susie asked if it would be okay for her to bring some of his ashes to scatter in front of The Arc.

"Yes," I replied, "out under the big sky, looking to the long horizon."

It has been said that my friend Hal was an architect. Yes, that is true. But a persuasive argument can be made that he was also a poet, a painter, and a piper—as his creations are in equal measure rhythmic, picturesque, and lyrical. I know. I am fortunate to live in one. And when I miss him, all I need do is walk around, for though he has now slipped out of form, he has generously left behind the beautiful contours of his imagination.

The Ambassadors

I had intended to arrive at my new home in the desert during the day, but got caught up attending to various tasks and arrived after dark. Unfortunately, I did not have a flashlight in the car, so the journey to the front door was a bit of a challenge—not only on account of the darkness, but because my arms were full of things friends had given me, insisting I carry them across the threshold upon entering my house for the first time: bread and salt (Jewish tradition), braided sweetgrass (Aleut), corn (Navajo). I found the lock and turned the key.

Setting everything down, I turned on the light in the entryway and discovered, right there at the threshold, Snake. He rose up a bit as I knelt down. I told him I was very glad that I had not stepped on him. He looked at me and slowly slithered away.

That night, I was lying in bed reading when I heard something flying back and forth in front of the bedroom window. *What flies at night? Do I have a bat?* I turned off the light and stepped outside. The moon was full, and I saw something fly right at me. It landed on the stucco column outside the bedroom, about a foot away from where I was standing: Red-shafted Flicker, a member of the woodpecker family. He looked at me and flew off.

The next morning, I took a walk around the house and came to my water fountain, yet to be filled. The well of the fountain lies about two feet below ground level. There inside was Toad. She couldn't get out, so I scooped her up and put her on the ground. She looked at me and hopped away. I found some scraps of sandstone and built some steps inside the fountain, in case she should return.

What's going on?

When I bought the hill on which I live, long before I built the house, I sat down on a spot a bit below the crest. I sat with intention. I asked permission of whomever might be listening to build my home there. It was a partly cloudy day. There was a storm off in the distance. Upon asking my question, I heard thunder to the north. It echoed again and again, in the four directions. *A resounding yes,* I thought, *or maybe no.*

On that first morning in my new home, I surmised that these animals—Snake from the Earth, Flicker from the Sky, and Toad from the Water—were ambassadors sent to welcome me. After twenty years now, I am convinced that that was true.

Animals visit every day. Coyotes climb up the hill every morning to eat the dog chow I leave for them; Finches, Sparrows, Jays, Doves, Grosbeaks, Towhees, Phoebes, Juncos, Red-winged Blackbirds, and a congress of about forty raucous Ravens arrive to eat the birdseed; Squirrels, Rabbits, Chipmunks, and Lizards join for lunch; and the occasional Rattlesnake slides in to see what's up.

Several months after I moved in, some friends came out from New York to visit for a few days. Every morning, we'd go outside to do our exercises. On one of those days, I was doing some dishes, and was a bit delayed in joining them.

"Dean! You've got to come out here! A bird is caught in the net!"

The landscapers had spread native grass seed around the house, and then put down straw and some netting so that the seed would not be eaten by the birds, and would have a chance to root. After several weeks, I had picked up most of the netting, but not all.

I ran outside to see Pinyon Jay in a panic, flapping his wings, trying to rise from the netting in which he had entangled himself. My city friends were also in a panic, not knowing what to do. I went back into the kitchen, got a scissors, and returned outside.

"I know what to do. Please calm down."

My friends stood silent. Somehow, without giving it much thought, I stood about twenty feet from the bird, looked at him and silently told him that I was going to come over there and help. He stopped flapping his wings. Slowly, I walked to him, holding him in my gaze. He didn't move. I stooped down and very carefully placed my hand over him, holding his wings in. I lifted him gently, and cut the netting from his feet. Freed, he hopped onto the palm of my hand, looked at me for a moment, and took off into the air with a *caaa!*

A couple of years ago, I stepped outside to spread some birdseed and discovered a very small baby animal on the deck. He didn't even have his eyes open. I picked him up, trying to figure out what he was and where he came from. It couldn't have been far. But I found no nest. I carried him inside the house, heated up some milk, and fed him with an eyedropper. He liked it. I could feel his heart beat in the palm of my hand.

I took him back outside and continued the search. After a while, I heard squeaking from up above. There, in a light column, was the mother, with several other babies holding onto her—Pack Rat. *Oh, great,* I thought. *I've held the baby and his mother will reject him; besides that, I probably now have some deadly disease.* I carefully put him down on the deck and stepped away, all the while watching the mother. I told her I was sorry. After a moment, she scurried down the stucco column, scooped up the baby in her mouth, and ran away. (Oh, and I lived to tell the tale.)

One morning, while I was doing sit-ups outside, lying on a mat, Rabbit hopped right up beside me. She followed me with her gaze—up, down, up, down. She seemed mesmerized, and wouldn't leave even when I started laughing.

Then, one afternoon, while sitting outside with friends and gesticulating as I talked, Finch flew over and landed on my index finger. Sometime later, I found Beetle in the house. I scooped him up and took him outside, knelt down and placed him on a leaf. I stayed there for a while, watching him crawl around on the plant. As I was getting up, my sight moved forward. There, about three feet away, was Rattlesnake, all five feet of her, watching. I acknowledged her and slowly stepped back. She stayed for a while, and then made her way across the sand.

Why did Jay quiet down? Why did Pack Rat not reject her baby? Why didn't Rabbit hop away? Why did Finch fly to my finger? Why didn't Rattlesnake strike? I believe that in all five instances, and many others over the years, the animals I have encountered read my intention. I do not wish to harm them, and they know this. I am an animal, too. I have built my nest and created my boundary, requesting that they not cross it, and assuring them that, when outside, I shall respect them and their homes. They know this, too.

And so, we live on this hill together, in peace.

With Their Hands

There has always been something about wood that I like: the feel of it, the look, but mostly its smell, freshly cut. I remember begging my father as a boy to bring me some. Weeks went by; then, one day, he was late coming home from work. When he drove up the driveway, he honked the horn and yelled for me to come outside. I rushed to the car as he opened the trunk. And there, heaped on top of one another, were countless fragrant treasures: pieces of blond scrap wood from the local lumberyard. Besides a fishing rod and reel I had received a year or two earlier for my birthday, this was the *best* gift I'd ever gotten. We unloaded the cargo and stacked everything in the garage. The next day, I set to work making birdhouses.

My grandfather Harry was a cooper and a cartwright in the "old country," in the village of Konela, Ukraine. After several failed attempts, in 1922 he succeeded in leading his family—my grandmother Bessie, my father Edward, and my aunt Ida—in an escape from the anti-Jewish pogroms that swept the country. Antisemitic immigration laws in the US at the time prohibited Jews from Eastern Europe, so they settled for a while in Montreal, Canada, but ultimately made it to Wisconsin. America didn't need barrels and carts, so my grandfather became a glazier and mirror-maker, and my father was his assistant. They worked with their hands.

Years later, with a loan from the bank and my mom's dowry, my dad bought a small metal scrapyard in Oshkosh, which in time he diversified and built into a very successful business. In one generation, our family—with its origins as village craftsmen—became landed gentry.

More than anything, my father wanted me to get an education and become a professional. Thus, besides making some pretty clunky birdhouses, I knew nothing of craft.

*

About ten years ago, a crew arrived at my home in New Mexico to lay down a new roof. It was a three-week project under the searing desert sun. Whenever I have workmen at the house, I like to be with them as they accomplish their tasks. I enjoy learning from them and doing what I can to help out. Although I knew nothing about laying down single-ply roofing, at least I could carry supplies and sweep up.

At the end of the last day of work, standing outside by the trucks, I handed out envelopes containing tokens of my gratitude. Having composed a message of appreciation for their efforts on my behalf (and using Google to translate it), I announced that I wanted to make *un discurso*. The men fell silent and looked at me. I read my little speech in halting Spanish, which may not have made much sense, but they seemed to appreciate the effort.

Later that day, I received a telephone call from the owner of the company expressing his appreciation for the regard with which I treated his men: "No one shows them that kind of respect. They won't stop talking about it."

*

There is a sixty-foot tunnel behind my house that daylights at one end and has a fan at the other. The fan pulls the air through the tunnel and dumps it into the house through a series of vents. The intent was to use the thermal mass of the earth to cool the house. That worked for several years, but the summers have become hotter, and I decided to have a couple of mini-split air conditioners installed upstairs in my study. Two young guys arrived for the day to do the installation. I watched from my desk, and we talked as they climbed up and down the ladders. Around noon we broke for lunch, and I made sandwiches and introduced them to orange pop. While we were sitting in the kitchen one of them looked over at the refrigerator, on which I have a multitude of photographs of friends and relations.

"Who's that with you?" he asked, pointing at a picture.

"That's the actor Paul Newman." Blank look.

"And that?"

"That's Robert Redford." Blank look. I had to restrain myself from pulling out my DVD of *Butch Cassidy and the Sundance Kid*.

As the day progressed, we kept on with our conversation. When the installation was complete and they were done with their work, they did not leave. We continued talking. They were seen. They were heard. Perhaps this was a novelty for them. If so, I am saddened for us all. Arthur Miller (of whom I doubt they have heard) was right: "Attention must be paid."

*

There have never been workers out here who haven't had interests beyond the perimeter of their profession, and it is of those that I often inquire. A fellow arrived to install a new pump in my irrigation system; as I hung out with him, working belowground, he spoke of his passion for "Old Ironsides," formally known as the *USS Constitution*, named by George Washington and one of the six original frigates of the United States Navy. It is the world's oldest commissioned naval vessel afloat. Having visited her several times in Boston Harbor, and felt the sacredness of her decks, she is my favorite ship as well. I excused myself and went into the house, where I had tucked away a small piece of wood that had been removed from the ship during one of its restorations. I brought it out and gave the relic to him.

"Wow! I'm going to build a plexiglass box for this and put it next to the model I built of the ship. I can't wait for my son to see this! Thank you so much."

*

Some years later, a crew arrived to re-stucco the house. This was going to be a long project: six weeks. Every day I was out there, carrying equipment and toting supplies to them as they worked arduously in the desert heat. Only one of them spoke just a little English, and he became my translator when words needed to be spoken.

At noon every day, we sat under the eaves and had lunch. They all brought homemade burritos; mine were from the local grocery store, and microwaved. As time went by, they got used to my presence and would joke around in Spanish during our meal. I had no idea what they were saying, but enjoyed the camaraderie.

Along with their burritos, each man brought along a small bottle of hot sauce. One day, after some joking around (some of which I think had to do with me), one of them offered his bottle. *This,* I thought, *is a test.* I shook a few drops onto the palm of my hand and licked them off. Then I shook a substantial amount on my burrito and took a bite. There was silence as they watched and waited. I smiled at them. Before I knew it, outstretched arms confronted me with bottles of hot sauce and urging to try each of their favorites. In that moment, despite the differences in culture and language, we had created a brotherhood.

When the project was done, my translator approached me and said, "You are a good man." That alone was worth the sunburn.

*

Having made it through university and earned a PhD in psychology and practiced and taught, I have mostly worked with my mind over the years. But I have always had a deep respect for those who work with their hands. There is something that binds us together. We all work with our hearts.

EXTENDING THE PERIMETER

"I won't be the first to let go."

The Tree I Planted

"Hey, neighbor!"

Gary and Eric, carrying the largest ice chest I had ever seen, rounded the corner and appeared at the open garage door. I had just arrived from New York at my new home in New Mexico, a small adobe house on Chimaja Hill in the village of Corrales, just across the Rio Grande from Albuquerque. I was sorting through boxes.

"Well, hello, I'm Dean."

"Oh, we know who you are. I'm Gary, and this is my son, Eric."

Something else they knew was that I did not yet have a refrigerator: that ice chest contained much-appreciated food.

That was the very beginning of friendships that have lasted the rest of my life. Soon, I met Gary's wife Glenda, and their daughter Stephanie. As time went by and we became close, they all insisted that I was family, and that they loved me—a word they often use, and mean every time. I initially resisted, but eventually surrendered and settled into their warm embrace.

One day, Glenda—an optimistic, sunny, quirky gal who couldn't resist a stray—introduced me to a puppy she had found abandoned in a parking lot. Their dog didn't get along with her.

"Maybe you could take her?"

"You know, I just got to New Mexico, and I'd really like to be free to travel around a bit before getting a dog."

"We could keep her at the house while you're away. Maybe she could just come by this afternoon for a visit."

Within Glenda was a lot of Glinda, the Good Witch of the North in *The Wizard of Oz*. She cast only good spells. Resistance was futile. And so the dog came by. She stayed seven years. I called her Sam, as that name came to mind the moment we met.

Soon thereafter, when I started reading stories to preschool kids at the community library every Wednesday morning, I was always on the lookout for good books. There was a magazine rack at the grocery store that sometimes had large paperbacks for kids. One day, while shopping, I wandered over there to take a look, and found *Sam the Dog.* Wow! What a coincidence. I opened the book, and to my astonishment discovered the story was about a dog named Sam and a boy named Dean. What are the chances?

To give Sam a safe place, I designed a fenced-in area. Eric came over to help build it, wearing bright white sweatpants and sweatshirt. By the end of our project, needless to say, those clothes bore significant sullied evidence of our arduous labors. Young people don't always make the best choices. We laugh about it now—as we also do about that time, not very long ago, when we were standing in my kitchen and I kept asking him to repeat himself.

"When was the last time you had your hearing checked!" he remarked. Although that stung a bit, I felt the love. And not long afterward, for the benefit of all, I got hearing aids.

When Eric married Heidi on a snowy day in December up in Michigan, he asked me to stay with him as he dressed for the ceremony. I remember helping him with his tie and put on his cufflinks—one of the true honors of my life. My favorite picture from those wedding days, besides the one where Heidi has draped a portion of her veil over Eric's head, is of Eric and me feeding each other cereal in the kitchen one winter morning. Some time later, they asked me to be godfather to their two exquisite kids, Jase and Mia.

Several years later, Glenda began to suffer from dementia, and as the disease slowly progressed, Gary would not leave her side. I have never witnessed such abiding devotion, patience, endurance, and—above all—*love* from one human being to another. When she passed away, he asked that I deliver the eulogy. As Glenda was one of the kindest, most generous, and compellingly good people I'd ever met, it was an honor to speak of her at that gathering of friends and family, all of whom adored her.

Not long afterward, Gary's brother Steve was in a car accident. Totally paralyzed, he was able only to blink his eyes. Gary and I immediately went up to Denver to the hospital to see him. We met up with Steve's dearest friends, and over many difficult days considered the options. The doctors were very careful with us, but also direct. There was nothing that medicine could do for his condition. Steve would develop systemic infections, which the hospital would treat, but then he would need to be discharged and placed in assisted living, where he would probably develop more infections and then be re-hospitalized … and that would become the rhythm of his life.

It was an agonizing time for everyone. We decided to consult with Steve. One of his friends met with him alone. Steve could communicate by blinking *yes* and *no*. When the situation was explained to him, he made it clear that he did not want to live this way, and agreed to the withdrawal of food and water. Shortly thereafter, he died.

A couple of years later, Stephanie and Tony fell in love, and she asked that I officiate the wedding. And so, I joined the likes of The Beatles and Lady Gaga, and got myself ordained online. I stood before them and our families, speaking and listening to the words that bound them together under the New Mexico sky.

The ensuing years have been filled with happy rendezvous and escapades, celebrations and much good cheer, all the more precious for what we have lost along the way.

How were we to know on that hot summer day in my garage that the coming years would be filled with such an abundance of both joy and sorrow? This is what happens when people choose to become family. You stand in the sun. You stand in the shadows. You stand together.

*

My friend Patty's nephews and niece, Will, Charlie, and Halle, are very dear to me. When they were growing up in New Jersey and I lived in New York City, we had a chance to spend time with each other. I missed them when I moved to New Mexico, but whenever I'd visit Manhattan, we'd get together. However, as they entered their teens, their lives became busy.

A couple of years ago, when I was in the city, we tried to put our schedules together—but it looked like it wasn't going to happen that time. One afternoon during that visit, after seeing a matinée with Patty and our friend Helen, we wandered around Greenwich Village and Chelsea, just randomly turning right and left, searching for a restaurant. My back began to give out, and I blurted: "Hey, I'm in some pain here. Why don't we just decide where we're going and get a cab?"

Their immediate and sincere concern for me made me uncomfortable: "Never mind. I'll be okay. Let's just make a decision and walk there." We chose a restaurant close by and continued on our way, then came to an intersection and turned right.

I saw them first. Walking toward us were Will, Charlie, Halle, and their folks Elizabeth and Bill. Then, in unison: "Oh, my God!"

Turns out it was Bill's birthday, and the family had come into the city for dinner. Thus we all trooped off together for a meal. Had they left their house two minutes earlier, or later … had we turned a different corner, as we aimlessly wandered through the Village … had we gotten into a cab … well, you know the rest. What are the chances?

*

Not long ago, a brand-new child arrived, occupying a point in the universe never occupied before and never to be occupied again: my friends Kelli and Eben's son Rory. A great blessing. Huzzah! And though I am old, from deep within arose a strength I did not know I had, called forth on behalf of a child. When he fell asleep on my chest, it crossed my mind: *This is why I am here.*

*

Love arises of itself, offering safe haven and emancipation from the captivity of fear and anger and sadness. Those distortions of spirit dissolve in its presence. So, too, does ego, it seems. I know this to be true when I am with those on the branches of my 'other' family tree—the tree I planted.

On that tree are brothers and sisters, nieces and nephews, and many children, kin not by birth but by choice. Of the many blessings of chosen family in my life are the young people who are most important to me. When I see them, I don't perform, as I so often do, for the amusement of others or the ennoblement of self. All that pretense disappears, and I am disarmed. I adore them, and would do anything for them. And if that ain't love, well, I don't know what is.

The truth is, if we trace them back far enough, we shall discover that the branches of *all* our family trees touch and intertwine with one another. We are all related. Accordingly, we all have royal blood in our veins. Therefore every child should be treated as a king or a queen. When all is said and done, when I disappear from view and people, for a time, speak of me and of what I did in my life, I hope that it will be said that for a moment, I respectfully knelt before a child.

It always surprises me that anyone gives me a thought without my being right in front of them, demanding their attention. However, with these young ones of whom I speak, it is not uncommon for me to hear from them out of the blue, and then we'll settle into a marathon conversation, as it seems we can't get everything said in under three hours. It is curious to me that a young person would want to hang out together, and, even more so, remember something I might have said a long time ago. To be held in memory is one of the greatest gifts of all.

In his essay "How to Grow Old," Bertrand Russell cautions elders about the young: "You must not expect that they will enjoy your company." Actually, I take that to heart: I never want to intrude on young people, whose lives are full and active with their peers. Memories of my own youth, and the bubble in which my pals and I resided, a bubble beyond the perimeter of which adults were not welcome, keeps me honest on that score.

However, if there is some reason for me to still be around, it is to give something to those behind me on the trail, to build a bridge over rough terrain, to offer advice when sought, encouragement when needed, comfort when required—and my hand.

What is family? People who love one another, abide with one another, are witness to and participants in both the joys and sorrows of each other's lives. In the final analysis, the only reason we are here at all is to take care of one another, and especially the young—even those we do not yet know.

Every family begins when strangers meet.

Sale Canceled

When I first moved to the New Mexico desert, I became aware that there was a need for increased social services for young people in my county. Having had social-service as well as political experience, I proposed the creation of a Youth Advisory Council to be composed of both professionals in relevant fields and young people, who would voice their own concerns and help to guide our efforts.

A group of county officials and concerned citizens formed an exploratory committee and met every week, alternating at various homes for a meal and a discussion. One day, while meeting at Becky's house, her eleven-year-old son Gabe came through the room and we talked for a bit about what interested him—art. As young people often do, he got right to the point: "You wanna see some of my paintings?"

Becky nodded her approval.

"Well, yes. After our meeting, I'll come up."

We had our meeting, and then Becky and I went to Gabe's room, where he showed me some of his very accomplished watercolors, many of which reflected Native American themes. We talked about what they meant to him.

As the months went by, every time we rotated our meeting over to Becky's, Gabe invited me to see his current work. One day, he showed me a small painting of a *kachina*, which he had set aside.

"You wanna have this one?"

"I would be honored to have it. Will you sign it for me?"

Using a straight edge, he drew a pencil line in the lower right corner, "to help me write straight."

The advisory council was a success. Our committee handed it off to others to run, and I went off to university to teach.

Years went by.

One day, while out in the garage, I came upon a box of old newspaper clippings—one of which contained an article about Gabe and his art, when he was an older teenager.

I went to the computer and did a search. At that very moment, he was having a one-man show at a gallery just outside of Albuquerque.

Although I probably should have called first, in my enthusiasm I just got into the car and made the hourlong drive. When I arrived at the gallery, it was closed. I peered through the windows and saw Gabe's work on the walls.

"Can I help you?"

I turned around. An older gentleman approached me from the parking lot.

"I don't think so. I wanted to visit the gallery, but I see that they're closed."

"Oh, you want to see Gabe's paintings? Come with me."

We walked around the adobe building, where the gentleman pulled out a key and opened the door.

"Hey, Rob, this guy wants to see Gabe's work."

It turned out that Rob—the man's son—owned the gallery, and had closed it for the day to take inventory.

"Great. Let me turn on some lights."

And so I got a one-man tour of the one-man show.

A painting of a couple of bears caught my attention, and my imagination. Gabe's palette was identical to what it had been as a child. "I'd like to buy this," I said.

"Done."

"I knew Gabe when he was just a boy. Would you deliver a note to him?"

"Sure. Here's some paper."

Several days later, I received a telephone call from Gabe. We decided to meet up for lunch. Just before he hung up, he said: "I want to thank you. You started me on my spiritual journey."

At lunch, we had a long conversation about how we had occupied our lives since the last time we had met, almost twenty years earlier. He told me how meaningful our little visits were to him when he was a boy. There wasn't anything in particular that I had said, but apparently just talking with him and listening to what was important to him back then had set him on a quest toward a deeper understanding of life.

I had brought along the *kachina* painting, which he was delighted to see. I also brought along my new acquisition: the bears painting.

"Will you sign it for me?"

"Hah! I always forget to do that."

We went to his car, where he had a small brush and a tube of paint. He didn't need a straight edge. Then we hugged and promised to stay in touch.

When I got to my car, I saw the parking ticket flapping under the windshield wiper, for $25. *Oh well*, I thought; *I guess our conversation lasted longer than I had anticipated.* I pocketed the ticket and drove off.

Noticing that I was low on gas, I pulled into a filling station and slid my card into the slot. The screen told me to select a grade and start pumping, which I did. I couldn't help but notice that the meter did not run while the gas flowed. When the tank was full, I put the pump handle back in its place. The screen said: SALE CANCELED.

I went into the shop and explained the situation to the clerk. Their register had no record of the sale. "I guess you just got a free tank of gas. Have a nice day."

Given the number of gallons I had pumped, I estimated it would have cost, well, about $25.

It was, indeed, a nice day.

Bella Italia

In the summer of 1998, I traveled to Italy with seven friends. One of the young couples had discovered a villa for rent in Tuscany. They arrived first, and when the rest of us drove up to the house, they had dinner prepared for us under the trees. Eating *al fresco* is really the only way to have a meal, especially in *Bella Italia*.

We began each day by getting into our three little cars and driving to a nearby town to get fresh food for breakfast, to add to the figs we picked from the trees on the property. Each of us was assigned to a particular item. One morning, it was my job to pick up some sweet rolls. I went into a café and approached the large glass case.

I pointed to the fresh-baked delicacies. "*Buongiorno. Uno ... uno ... uno.*"

As in many such cafés throughout Italy in the early mornings, there were beautifully dressed Italians stopping by on their way to work, standing at tall, tiny tables, sipping their coffees, and reading their newspapers.

I felt someone watching me, and turned to my right. In the corner of the room was a stunning woman who I could have sworn was Sophia Loren in her younger years. She smiled at me and said something. I couldn't hear her, and even if I could, I do not speak Italian. But her hand gestures and her expressions made clear her inquiry: *How can you eat so many pastries and stay so slender?*

We both laughed. No translation necessary.

As I say, I don't speak Italian. But, I do know one sentence in that language, and in several others: *I am happy to see you. "Sono felice di vederla."* I have always been good at mimicry (a skill that would often drive my dear mother to distraction when I would parrot back to her what she said, exactly as she said it), and could pronounce that phrase quite well.

Once a week, a woman would come to the villa to change the towels and sheets. When she first arrived, I greeted her with the phrase. She was utterly delighted, and responded with a torrent of Italian—none of which I understood. Pointing to my mouth and shaking my head,

I made clear that I could neither understand her nor respond. She laughed; I laughed. No translation necessary.

From our villa, we could see the towers of the medieval town of San Gimignano. Whenever I looked at them, I felt uncomfortable. However, my friends wanted to take a day trip there. One day after breakfast, we got in the cars to make the drive. The closer we came to the town, the more discomfort I felt in my body, the more dread. I knew nothing about San Gimignano, and couldn't think my way out of this physical reaction. By the time we reached it, I was feeling both ill and disoriented.

"You all go explore," I told the others. "I'll just sit here on this bench." And that is where I remained for the next couple of hours, with my eyes closed. On the drive back home, my friends asked how I was, and what was wrong. I couldn't explain what had happened, but as each mile passed between us and that town, I began to feel better.

Once back in the States, I read about San Gimignano. There are many theories about those towers—some quite sinister, involving blood feuds. But I didn't know that when I was there.

As the serene village of Assisi is special to me—my favorite of the saints is Francis—I decided to take the train there for a day by myself, before my friends joined me. I had been there thirteen years earlier, and re-walked the paths and revisited its many churches. When my friends drove up the main road into town the following day, I greeted them as if Assisi were my own. We had a wonderful time exploring that beautiful village over the next couple of days, including the basilica where Saint Francis was laid to rest.

One day, on my own, I climbed to the top of the hill. On the other side below me was a road, beside which I saw a pile of rocks. I climbed down toward it and discovered a multitude of rose-colored stone chips, most probably left by a mason who had crafted stones to build a house. Most of the dwellings in Assisi are made of this stone, and they glow at dawn. I looked around to see if anyone was near who might claim ownership of these chips. There was no one. I thought it might be okay for me to take some, and into my pockets they went. Over the years I have given them away, and everyone's response is the same. They silently rub the chip and then smell it: a bit of Assisi in the palm of their hand.

After about ten days at the villa, we traveled south to Rome. Once there, besides noticing that the traffic signals are simply suggestions, we became completely lost on our way to the hotel. We parked at the side of the road and took out our map. A young man on a Vespa with his girlfriend pulled over to us.

"Can I help?"

We told him where we were headed, and he said he knew how to get there and to just follow him. When we arrived at the hotel, we called out *"Grazie!"* and waved a bottle of wine toward him as a gift, as he sped away. His girlfriend turned around to us, smiling, and waved her finger back and forth: *No. No.* We still speak of "Scooter and His Girlfriend," and their kindness.

While in Rome, we trekked to Vatican City to see St Peter's Basilica. Having climbed the many steps to the entrance, six of us were allowed in—but my friend Ryan and I were stopped by a rather officious young man in an ill-fitting suit who told us we could not enter because we were not wearing long trousers. I wanted to tell him that, while he could see my Bermuda shorts, he could not discern my earnest intent. However, I thought it would be best to remain silent and surrender to the dress code. What he might have said to a certain man in a robe and sandals in an earlier age also crossed my mind.

My friend and I retreated to the plaza, where we contrived a scheme: we would return to the city to buy some trousers to rent out to others who were barred entry from St Peter's. That gave us a laugh. But we simply returned the following day, properly attired, and experienced the shrinking feeling of entry into a cathedral the scale of which is unimaginably huge. We felt like ants as we crossed the floor.

Guidebook in hand, I began to look around at the splendid stained glass, sculptures, mosaics, and paintings. Yet I could find no depiction of Francis of Assisi in the cathedral, as important as he is in the communion of saints. I approached a guard and asked if he could direct me to an image of Francis. He looked puzzled and took me to another guard, whose response was the same. They knew of none. Francis gave up all worldly possessions. Perhaps his presence in such a majestic place would be unseemly.

The Sistine Chapel, with its ceiling fresco of Creation painted by Michelangelo, astonished us with its power. It is in this room in conclave (that is, "under lock and key") that cardinals assemble to elevate one of their own to the papal throne.

Years later, I boarded a plane; sitting next to me was a young priest. I happened to be wearing black jeans, a black sweater, and a white shirt. "So, this is where they put those of us in black and white," I said. He was not amused. However, during the flight, we did engage in a bit of conversation, and I inquired about the process of papal election, pointing out that, after the most liberal Pope John XXIII, the College of Cardinals elected Paul VI, an ardent conservative.

"How much politicking occurs during the conclave?" I asked.

"None. It is all decided by the Holy Spirit."

Fascinating.

The vast majority of our recollections of that trip to Italy are happy: living in our own villa, exploring neighboring vineyards, going on morning expeditions to nearby towns and daytrips to Sienna and Florence, languid days in Assisi and Rome, the welcoming sight of the appealing weather-beaten, burnt-orange stucco that coats so many ancestral Italian buildings … all impressed themselves deeply into memory, informed by the wise Italian tradition of *il dolce far niente* ("the sweetness of doing nothing").

Whenever we entered a restaurant in Italy, we would say to the host, "*Otto persone*" ("Eight people")—and to this day, that is how Hal, Susan, Ryan, Cindy, Kelli, Erin, Carol, and I refer to ourselves. And each time we do, a flood of memories bathes us, and we return to *Bella Italia* and the embrace of its generous people.

Returning

When I first arrived in New York City in the summer of 1976—an escapade that was to last thirteen years—I left my apartment to wander around the neighborhood. There on MacDougal Street was the famous Caffe Reggio, a coffeehouse first opened in 1927 in the heart of Greenwich Village. In the 1950s, the Beat Generation writers and artists gathered—people such as Jack Kerouac, Allen Ginsberg, and William S. Burroughs; later, in the 1960s, folksingers such as Bob Dylan, Joan Baez, and Judy Collins gathered here as well.

When I stepped off the bright sidewalk into the cool darkness of the café, I noticed how crowded it was. However, there was one very small, unoccupied white circle amongst the crowd. I headed over to the table.

"May I help you?"

"A double espresso, please." While I waited for the cup's arrival, I opened my journal to write of my experiences so far in the big city. In a few minutes, the waiter returned with my coffee. I drank it, drinking in the atmosphere as well.

The following day, I returned. Again, it was very crowded. And again, that little white table invited. I sat down.

"May I help you?"

"A double espresso, please."

I wrote and sipped.

The day after that, I returned. Again, it was very crowded, and again, much to my amazement, that very same little white table was unoccupied. As I sat down, the waiter approached with a double espresso.

I had arrived.

Many years later, while traveling in Europe with friends, we reached the city of Heraklion on the island of Crete and toured around. As evening fell, we searched for a restaurant and found a brightly lit eatery off the main street. We walked past the dozen or so tables to a glass case at the end of the room, where we pointed to various dishes that were to be our meals.

The following day, rather tired after visiting archaeological sites, we were again confronted with choosing a restaurant.

"Why don't we just go back where we had dinner last night?"

"Oh well, okay." And so, we returned, walked to the glass case and selected our dishes.

The day after that, having been on our feet all day long, we were pretty exhausted.

"Where should we have dinner?"

"I say we go back."

"Really? There's got to be another place."

"Come on. It was good."

And so, we returned. When we got to the glass case, the owner looked at us and smiled, recognizing his devoted diners. We selected our dishes and, as we turned to go to our table, he said: "No. Come," and gestured for us to follow him back into the kitchen. It was there, amongst his friendly family, where we ate our dinner.

From Crete we went to Athens, and amongst the many ancient sites there, we climbed the Acropolis to the Parthenon. It captivated me. Every day thereafter, when my friends boarded their tour buses to visit other places, I returned to that magnificent building and sat, looking at it and drawing it in before I drew it out onto paper. I sat there in the sunlight, in the rain, and even once at night, when I snuck onto the top of the hill.

Today I can close my eyes, and I am sitting at the base of the Parthenon, eating family dinner at the restaurant in Crete, sipping espresso at Caffe Reggio. There is something reassuring about returning to a familiar place. And although I suppose I have missed out on a variety of experiences in my life as a result, I wouldn't have it any other way.

Annika in the Snow

It was late December 2000 when I boarded my flight from Albuquerque to New York City. Although it was rather mild in the New Mexico desert, I had heard that an enormous storm was descending on New York. My flight connected in Houston, and by then I knew what was up ahead: a huge blizzard, promising at least a foot and a half of snow in Manhattan.

Sitting next to me on that second flight was a young woman of about twenty who had been on a US tour with an international choir. For one reason or another, the tour had been canceled midway through, and she was headed to New York to then take a train upstate to stay with friends before returning to Germany.

At one point she got up, and I noticed a tattoo in the small of her back. When she returned, I asked her about it. "It's a Chinese symbol for *long life*," she replied, and so we started talking about philosophy and spirituality. As is often the case with the young, passionate opinions were expressed; and as is often the case with the old, tempered responses were given. The conversation was most enjoyable and animated.

Given the snowstorm, I asked Annika where she was going to stay in the city.

"Oh, I'll just sleep in a chair at the airport."

"Um, no, I really can't let that happen."

"But I don't have the money for a hotel room."

"Okay, I know this is strange, but here is my suggestion: you and I shall go to my hotel, and I shall provide you with your own room for the night. And then, tomorrow evening, you can be on your way to your friends upstate."

"Really?"

We made an agreement then and there.

When we arrived at John F. Kennedy International Airport, the blizzard was ferocious, but we were able to get a cab and head into town.

Upon arrival at The Wyndham, I approached the desk and asked for an additional room.

"I'm sorry, sir, but because of the storm, many guests who were supposed to check out haven't done so. We have no more rooms."

After calling several other hotels and hearing the same story, I called my dear friend Patty, who lives on the Upper West Side.

"Patty, I have a young gal here who needs a place to stay the night. Is your spare room available?"

"Of course; bring her over."

Annika and I got into another cab in Midtown, and slowly traveled up through the blinding snow.

Once I got Annika settled at Patty's, with a promise that I would return the following morning and take her around the city—which she had never seen—I returned to my hotel and went to bed. It had been, after all, a long day.

The next day, the sun was out and the blizzard had stopped, leaving behind about eighteen inches of glistening, pristine powder throughout the city. I took the subway uptown and picked up Annika. She was very excited to see New York. We went to Rockefeller Center to see the magnificent Christmas tree, to Times Square, down to Greenwich Village to see Washington Square and stop for coffee at the famous Caffe Reggio. We got enormous slices of pizza at Ray's and ate them as we tromped through the snow. For me, it was like having a daughter and showing her my town.

That evening, I took her to the train station for her trip upstate. I stood on the platform as her train departed. She hung out the window, waving, smiling, and crying. I waved and smiled and cried and watched until she disappeared.

Upon returning to my hotel, the desk clerk said, "Dr Rudoy, there's a package for you."

I received the small parcel and went upstairs to my room. Upon opening it, I found a beautiful letter from Annika accompanying a small box, within which was a gold and onyx charm inscribed on one side with the Chinese symbol for *long life*, and on the other, the symbol for *good fortune*.

Damned at the Wedding

The wedding took place on a patch of grass under the sun, with the desert laid out and the mountains rising in the distance. The young couple stood there, shy but confident, their hands touching as they were joined by the minister. A hundred or so family and friends witnessed them, sitting on white folding chairs. Afterward, we slowly made our way up the hill into the hall for the post-nuptial dinner.

*

I had known the groom, the son of a dear friend of mine, since he was a young boy, and had watched him grow into a good and decent man. We had many conversations over the years. When he was young and didn't yet know about propriety, he would sometimes just show up at my door: "Can we talk?" I'd get some lemonade or soda out of the refrigerator, and we'd sit outside and talk about, well, pretty much everything. He had a lot of questions, and thought I had a lot of answers.

Our conversations often veered into philosophical and spiritual realms of mystery and speculation. As he grew older, and the lessons of his fundamentalist Christian education began to take hold, he struggled to maintain a connection with me as the circle of his beliefs began to shrink. We did not speak of this directly; I just remained where I always was, present and available to him, hoping that that consistency and continuity would be enough to bridge the growing differences in our life views.

That's not to say that we didn't test the boundaries. He had known for years that I am gay. I asked him once what his congregation thought about homosexuality, and whether or not the subject ever came up in the group for which he served as youth minister.

"Hate the sin. Love the sinner," he replied.

"Oh, so you are being taught to hate."

He fell silent. So did I. The point had been made. After a minute or so of running our fingers along the condensation building up on our glasses of lemonade, we moved onto other topics.

Then there was the conversation about Jews for Jesus. One or two of his friends belonged to this group. He asked me, "Being Jewish, what do you think of them?"

"Well, being Jewish doesn't mean I am either 'for' or 'against' Jesus. However, one of the fundamental characteristics that defines a Christian is the belief in the exclusive divinity of Jesus. That is a threshold of belief that Jews do not cross. Those who do, become Christians. There is no middle ground. So, I don't quite understand why these former Jews, now converted to Christianity, would call themselves 'Jews for Jesus,' except to be provocative."

I think my young friend might have been disappointed at this response. Perhaps he thought he had discovered a common ground of belief on which we both could stand. Perhaps he wanted to 'save' me.

As time went by and he grew older, accumulating more responsibilities and demands on his time, we met less often. But somehow, that didn't matter. Whenever we did meet up, we always picked up just where we'd left off. There were times when he reminded me of things I had told him many years earlier, which continued to have an impact on his life. I don't know if he ever realized how deeply that moved me. Somehow, he had been able to accommodate in his heart both what he had learned from me and what he had learned from his church—despite, at times, the diametrically opposed nature of these opinions. Certainly, there was common ground, as there always is between people who care for one another.

*

The couple had honored me by seating me with the bride's family. There were toasts and laughter, and a few tears. Dinner was served. A young cousin of the bride sat to my left. We struck up a conversation. He told me that he wanted to serve in the military as a spiritual counselor.

"Oh, have you studied that formally?"

"Yes, I'm getting my degree."

"You must have had to study many different belief systems to be prepared for the variety of religious traditions you'll find amongst those in the military."

"No."

Now, this answer should have told me what was up ahead, but I blithely continued: "Have you had some experience out in the field?"

"Yes, I went on a couple of missions."

"That must have put your education to the test. Did your hands-on work with people in their communities begin to reshape what you'd learned in the classroom?"

"No."

Again, a door shut in my face, which I chose to ignore.

We skirted around the issue of our own personal belief systems, but I told him just a little bit about what I thought regarding the commonalities amongst religions. He listened politely. When I was through, he looked directly at me and said: "If you do not accept Jesus Christ as your Lord and Savior, you will be condemned to the fires of Hell for all Eternity."

I felt my jaw drop.

This young man's father, sitting across the table, beamed with pride at his son's proclamation. I was enraged—not at the son, but at the father, for being so proud of what he had done: closed shut his son's mind and heart. I was sad for the son, that a young person on the threshold of adulthood, with the full promise that only youth can bring, would be so narrow in his life's trajectory.

However, I have hope for him, that one day he will open his fist of belief and become acquainted with the doubt hidden within it. He might yet outgrow his father's house.

*

About a year later, my friend and I were sitting outside, drinking lemonade and reminiscing. I told him about my conversation at the wedding table with his wife's cousin. When I quoted the young man's condemnation, my friend said: "He doesn't get it."

"No. But if he's lucky, he will."

Pain's Antidote

I had been in pain for some time. The x-ray showed disintegration of the articular cartilage at the lumbosacral joint of my spine. Two discs were rubbing against one another. Diagnosis: degenerative disc disease. The inflammation manifested as occasionally severe sciatica down both legs.

The diagnosis eased my mind. There's nothing like a *name* to focus one's attention. Learning that this condition was not uncommon during the eighth decade of one's life also alleviated a good deal of anxiety.

I have good days and bad, and I know immediately upon awakening which it's going to be. Pain has become my companion, and I have made a certain peace with him. As long as I do my morning regimen of stretching exercises, I can usually keep him at a cordial distance.

A family of six was coming over for lunch. I awoke in pain that morning and thought perhaps I ought to postpone our rendezvous, but I really didn't want to cancel on them, and decided to power through as best I could.

When they arrived at the front door, I got on my knees to embrace the three children, whom I have known since their births. We all started talking at once and made our way to the kitchen, where I served spaghetti and salad. We sat down at the table and enjoyed our meal, seasoned with stories and laughter. I had set out some art supplies, and the kids got to it after lunch, scattering glitter everywhere while we grown-ups continued our conversation. They all stayed for about four hours.

When they were getting ready to leave, the eldest child asked, "Can I get a hug?" And I fell to my knees to provide the embrace, which was joined immediately by the other two kids. It felt good.

When they left, and I was at the sink rinsing dishes, I realized I was in significant pain. Even standing was a challenge.

It crossed my mind that, most probably, I had been in pain during the entire visit, but was not aware of it because my attention was elsewhere. Love is a powerful antidote.

It is useful to recall the advice of *Star Wars* Jedi Master Qui-Gon Jinn to his student Obi-Wan Kenobi: "Your focus determines your reality."

And so it did.

Touching

During my psychology internship in the early 1980s at Bellevue Hospital in New York City, most of my time was tightly scheduled with seminars as well as inpatient and outpatient work. However, there were occasionally openings during the week, and I could wander around the hospital. At one such time, I asked a highly regarded surgeon if I might accompany him and his medical residents on rounds. He agreed.

We arrived at the door of a private room. The surgeon told us that the elderly patient within would be lying on her back because of her condition, and that when we entered, we should remain at the threshold while he spoke with her. He opened the door, and we all quietly stepped in.

Instead of stopping at the foot of her bed to pull the silver metal clipboard containing her chart and study it, which I had seen many surgeons do, he proceeded directly to her. He knelt beside the bed so that his face was close to hers, and asked her how she was doing. They spoke quietly for several minutes; all the while, his hand was on her arm. Then he told her he was going to look at her chart. She nodded. He rose, gently pulled the chart out, and read it. He wished her well and promised to return the following day, opened the door, and we left the room. I had never witnessed such compassion before from a surgeon. But, of course, he was more than that: he was a healer.

Some years later, I had to have surgery at the same hospital. I was given a sedative and placed on a gurney, which was wheeled down the long hallways to the operating room. I still remember the blinding glare of the fluorescent lights overhead as we made our way through the corridors. Apparently, we arrived early, so they left me lying outside the OR, staring up at the lights, alone. The sedative was taking effect, and I began to feel somewhat disoriented. I started to worry that maybe they had taken me to the wrong operating room; maybe the wrong surgery was going to be performed; maybe I was going to die.

Some minutes passed, during which my fears mounted. And then I heard voices approaching from behind. I wanted to get up. I wanted to say something. But I couldn't move or speak. Two nurses stopped at the head of the gurney. They were talking about what they were going to do over the weekend. Then one of them rested her hand on my forehead and began to stroke it, while describing, to her friend, her plans to go camping with her boyfriend. She said nothing to me. In fact, her petting me seemed rather impersonal. However, that touch, skin to skin, completely dissolved my fear. I was not alone.

Some years ago, my friend Kate Linder was being honored with the placement of a star on the Hollywood Walk of Fame for her acting and years of philanthropic work. A bunch of pals came to Los Angeles from as far away as New York and London. We had met about twenty-five years earlier, when we all lived in Manhattan, and although we'd scattered over the years, we remained close. We all took rooms at the famed Roosevelt Hotel. A couple of hours before the ceremony, we gathered in my room and ended up on the bed, just hanging out with one another. It came time for us to get on with the schedule, but no one wanted to leave the comfort of our collective—the warmth of our contact.

Some time later, while walking briskly east on 96th Street in Manhattan, I encountered a father and his young son ahead of me. I smiled and nodded as I passed them. After a little while, the father passed me without the boy, who had apparently become distracted along the way. Suddenly, I felt a small hand in mine. The boy had run to catch up with his dad, and had apparently mistaken me for him. He looked up at me, a little startled, but then he smiled and ran after his father. It was only a moment, but somehow very important.

Not long ago, during the coronavirus pandemic, I went to lunch at the home of my friends Jonathan and Shaila. I've known Jon since he was a boy, and have known their three children—Noah, Levi, and Malaika—since birth. During our meal, each of the kids at one time or another came up to me, excited to show me something they had made, or something from their collections. In each instance, to keep us safe, I had to hold out my arm and remind them not to get too close. It was heartbreaking. They were old enough to understand what was going on, but in their natural enthusiasm, they forgot. As much as we grown-ups need to touch and be touched, for children, it is essential. Touching is a reminder that all is well, that there is safe harbor.

When this crisis passes, I thought, *I shall look forward to their hugs. I know I won't be the first to let go.*

AS LUCK WOULD HAVE IT

"The gift was used. I keep it shined."

Shylock's Star

Before I begin this story, you need to know about something that happened to me when I was in junior high school. My class took a field trip from Oshkosh down to Milwaukee to see a performance of *The Merchant of Venice.* It was presented in the round, and we had seats right at the edge of the raised stage. It was thrilling to be so close to the actors, even to feel the spray of their spit as they marched across the stage, declaiming their lines.

At one impassioned moment, Shylock tore the Star of David from his cloak, the emblem of his Jewish identity that he was forced to wear. He threw it down—right into my lap.

During my childhood, I had a very active imagination. In fact, I lived my life partially in that realm and partially in what most people would agree is reality. Well, besides being in shock with a Star of David in my lap, I considered this to be a sign. But I wasn't sure of what.

Years later, in between my freshman and sophomore years at college, I went back home to Oshkosh to spend the summer of 1968 there. I had no particular plans—just to enjoy some time off from my studies.

I discovered that another local boy, Bob Sphatt, who had made it very big in New York City as a model, had also returned home, with some show-business friends in tow, to create the Wisconsin Music Theatre summer stock company. The plan was to construct a huge tent on the grass at Menominee Park at the edge of Lake Winnebago, and put on a series of shows. This would have been a grand plan, but for the fact that shortly after it was set up, the tent blew down in a storm. But the show must go on, so these intrepid New Yorkers searched the city for an alternative site and ultimately changed the venue to the Masonic Temple—where they constructed a stage in the center of a large room to put on shows in the round.

I was intrigued, so I went to their offices to see if I could volunteer to help out, maybe sweep up or take tickets or something. When I arrived and expressed my interest, the fellow in the office said: "What's your shoe size?"

"Nine and a half."

"Try these on." I slipped on the cowboy boots he'd passed me, and he said: "You want to join the company?"

"Um. Sure."

As suddenly as that, I was cast in *Oklahoma*, *Carousel*, and *Once Upon a Mattress*. I was a cowboy in the first two and a lord at court in the third, for which I traded in my boots for a pair of fuchsia tights and dance slippers, and grew a moustache and goatee.

Being a member of a summer stock company means you don't just act and sing and dance—you build costumes and sets. While you perform a show at night, during the day you rehearse the next show, which opens the night after the other one closes.

The company had rented an entire floor in a local hotel for the cast and crew. Every night, after curtain, we'd troop over there, take the elevator up, and spread out on the carpeted hallway floor outside their rooms. One of us would make a donut run, and we'd talk and laugh and eat the confections into the wee hours of the morning, at which time I'd drive home, take a quick shower, and climb into bed for a few hours before returning to work on sets and rehearse.

Creating something together with a group of performing artists and spending every waking moment in their company was pretty intense. I had never before experienced such intimacy; all those Academy Awards speeches that referred to the "family" that formed during a production began to make perfect sense. I loved these people, and they loved me. We became like brothers and sisters, and developed our own language and way of being. We lived in a sort of bubble—just theater people—and made art and served it to an appreciative community. It was pretty heady stuff.

When the summer ended and we struck the sets for the final time, we all hugged and cried and exchanged telephone numbers and addresses, fervently promising to stay in touch. I was naïve: I thought we would. I did write a couple of letters and received a couple in turn, but it all petered out after a month or so as everybody got on with their lives.

I understand now that that's the way it is with theater folk. They're nomads at heart, moving on, moving on. However, because the intimacy that was created in such an intensely collaborative effort didn't last beyond the final curtain doesn't mean it wasn't real. Indeed, those things in this life that are only temporary are the most precious things of all.

Years later, I moved to New York City. One day, I discovered that one of the summer-stock actresses was in a Broadway show. I went to see it, and after curtain, I went backstage to see her. We hugged and laughed and remembered that sunlit summer. We promised to stay in touch—but knew we wouldn't.

It Could Have Been No Other Way

Back in 1972, I served as Education Director of the National Committee for a SANE Nuclear Policy. This research and advocacy organization was founded in 1957 in response to the destabilizing effects of the nuclear arms race, and became a powerful voice for arms control and disarmament. Amongst its supporters were Eleanor Roosevelt, Norman Thomas, Dr Benjamin Spock, Lenore Marshall, A. Philip Randolph, Walter Reuther, and Coretta Scott King.

It was my responsibility to develop materials for distribution to Congress and the public. Initially, all these documents were in print, and I thought it would be even more effective to make a documentary film. So I spent countless hours in the Library of Congress researching American foreign and military policy. At last, I had a script and some ideas for the visuals. Next up, we needed a narrator. We approached Academy Award-winning screen legend Paul Newman and he agreed, suggesting that I should come to his home in Westport, Connecticut.

When I drove into his driveway and stepped out of the car, I was greeted by two enormous and very friendly Russian Wolfhounds, both of whom leapt up and landed their front paws on my shoulders.

"Hello! Are you Dean?"

Coming through a narrow passage between two hedges, beyond which there was a swimming pool, was Paul, in his swimsuit.

"Yes, I'm Dean. How do you do, Mr Newman?"

We shook hands; he told me to call him Paul, and said he'd go right in and change and we'd be on our way to the recording studio. A few minutes later, he came out of the house.

"Do you want to drive, or shall I?"

"Well, since you know where we're going, you take the wheel."

We got into his silver Porsche and sped on a country road to Weston, about a ten-minute drive, which we made in record time. Along the way we talked—mostly about car racing, which was his passion aside from making films. Upon arrival at the studio in the middle of the Weston woods, we climbed out of the car and Paul put his arm over my shoulder as we approached the small

A-frame building. There were some people climbing down the steps. When we met and made introductions, Paul said: "This is my friend Dean." He then explained to me that he needed to record a quick public-service announcement for these folks, and that then we could get down to business. When that was accomplished and they had left, I talked with the recording engineer and Paul about the project.

"Paul, I sent you the script. Have you had a chance to go through it?"

"No, but don't worry. It'll be fine."

A cold read. That spelled trouble.

I stepped nervously to the microphone to introduce the narrator briefly; Paul slipped behind me to a keyboard, and pounded out a fanfare. We all burst out laughing, and happily that broke the ice.

During his recording of the script, Paul would occasionally make a mistake, and I'd have to stop him: "Um, Paul, you skipped a couple of words in that third sentence. Can we take it from the top?"

"Oh, I'll just take it from the middle of that sentence."

From the middle of the sentence! Understand, this was long before digital recording. We were working with quarter-inch, reel-to-reel tape. How in the world was the engineer going to patch something into the middle of a sentence? Well, I was uncomfortable arguing with my new friend, so we proceeded.

After about an hour of work, the engineer's wife brought us bagels and beer, which we readily consumed. As more hours went by, we kept drinking. More mistakes were made and picked up midstream, just like that first time. It was a half-hour script, but took all afternoon to record, given the pick-ups and the beer. However, a lot of fun was had. We wrapped everything up, and Paul and I drove home.

As we got out of the car, Paul said: "Say, Joanne [Woodward, his then-equally famous film star wife] and I are having dinner tonight with Eli Wallach and Anne Jackson. Why don't you join us?"

By now, you would think, I would have been entirely comfortable with Paul—but I was still in some degree of shock at how immediately warm and friendly he was to me. Suddenly, I became very shy and insecure. I couldn't believe his invitation; why would he want me to join them? What would I say at dinner?

"Thank you so much," I replied, "but I really need to get back to Washington."

"Oh, too bad."

And so, I got into my rental and drove back to my motel, kicking myself all the way … and for the next fifty years. What an extraordinary opportunity I let slip away, all because I was afraid! Lesson learned … but not quite.

(By the way, when I received the finished tape from the engineer, it was perfect. Paul knew how good this guy was, and indeed, he was a master.)

*

About fifteen years later, my friend Nan was casting a theatrical piece in Greenwich Village in New York City for John Cassavetes, the actor, screenwriter, director, and pioneer of American independent film. She asked if I wanted to tag along for an audition one afternoon. Having never witnessed that process, I said yes. I arrived at the theater, and we waited for the appearance of the actor. He never showed.

"Let's go to the White Horse Tavern and have some lunch."

"Good idea."

We walked over and got a table outside. I went in to freshen up, and there, sitting at the bar, were John Cassavetes, his wife Gena Rowlands, and his actor friends Ben Gazzara and Peter Falk. When I returned to the table, I told my friend they were there, and asked: "Do you think it would be okay if I sent them a drink?"

"Are you kidding? He'd love that."

About twenty minutes later, they came outside and walked over to our table: "Hey, thanks for the drinks."

Introductions were made, and I noticed that John was staring at me, *studying* me. Suddenly, it became clear to me that he was under the impression that I was the actor auditioning for a role in his piece.

"Mr Cassavetes, I think you might think I'm an actor. I'm just a friend, and I'm studying to be a psychologist."

"I like psychologists."

"I like directors."

"You have a good voice. You should audition for the part."

Soon afterward, they left. "What just happened?" I asked.

"He wants you for the part."

"Wait, he said I should *audition* for the part."

"Look. That's the way he always works. He loves casting non-professionals as actors. They bring an edge of reality. Trust me. He wants you."

"Wow! But I'm in the middle of writing my dissertation. If I leave it now, I'm afraid I'll never get it done." Of course, that was *not* what I feared; I feared I would make a fool of myself, that I would disappoint him. "I need to sleep on this."

"Okay, but things move pretty quickly in this business. Let me know tomorrow."

The next day, I called her and said I'd have to pass on the opportunity. Although I felt relieved, I also felt enormous regret … a feeling that has endured for almost forty years.

*

Now in my seventies, retired from psychology, I have been recording audiobooks and doing some writing. In this encore career, in a way, I have finally made it to show business. But what might have happened along the way, at those lucky forks in the road where possibility beckoned? Sadly, I'll never know.

Recently, I was telling these stories of regretted moments, of lost opportunities, to my friend and acting coach Ellie. "I'm really sorry I didn't take those guys up on their offers. What fun it would have been."

She simply said: "It could have been no other way, or it would have been." It strikes me that that is one of the truest statements I have ever heard, and one of the most consoling. Yes, at those moments in time, for a host of reasons, I was not ready or able to take advantage of those opportunities offered. Now, when I think back at them, I understand that young man and his sins of both commission and omission over the years; although an explanation is no excuse, that softens the regret … at least a bit.

In any case, that was when I was young, when I permitted circumstances to compel my conduct. Now, I am old. I choose how to conduct my life. Sometimes I retreat into cowardice, and suffer the consequences of shame. Sometimes I advance with courage, and earn from the attempt a new sense of self-respect. Sometimes I have to fake it before I make it.

Eyes wide open, with an occasional glance in the rear-view mirror, I make my choice.

Surrender

Amongst my pals in junior high school, I was the first to change: where once stood a young tenor, suddenly and quite unexpectedly a lilting soprano appeared. This was a source of great embarrassment—until at last the change was complete. My new voice was deep and mellow, and I was often asked to speak, narrate, and serve as Master of Ceremonies at various school functions.

For the next fifty years, I employed my voice in various activities that commanded some degree of attention, and was often told it was pleasing to hear. In the back of my mind, I sometimes thought I might shape a career around it. Time went by, and life unfolded. At the age of sixty-five and somewhat retired, I decided to explore an encore career. But first, a little backstory:

When I was a boy, my parents had some LPs by comedians: Bob Newhart, Joan Rivers, Shelley Berman, Phyllis Diller, Alan Sherman … Sometimes my Aunt Libian and Uncle Ben, who lived just a couple of blocks away, would come over, and we'd sit and listen to these records. We used our imaginations; it was as if these guys were right there in the living room with us. And we laughed and laughed, no matter how many times we heard them.

My folks also had one record by Pearl Williams, a bawdy chanteuse and comedienne, which they kept hidden away in their bedroom night-table. Of course, I found it and listened to it once, when they were out with friends and I was home alone. I didn't quite understand what Williams was talking about, but I knew it was very naughty.

I myself owned several 45s of children's stories, which I still have. The records weren't opaque black discs but translucent red and yellow, like gemstones: *The Shoemaker and the Elves*, *Aladdin*, *Jack and the Beanstalk*, and Hans Christian Andersen's *The Red Shoes*. They were magical. I'd put one on my record player, lie down on the floor, close my eyes, and be transported to fantasy worlds by the narrator's voice.

Now retired, I thought of recording some children's stories that might enchant kids the way I had been enchanted, listening to those records. I cashed in a coupon for a voiceover class, and arrived at the appointed time at a building on Manhattan's Upper West Side. I was escorted down to the basement; there, in a little sound studio, were two other people and our teacher, a gal named Ellie. She was sporting a baseball cap, and I liked her immediately.

After a bit of conversation about why we were all there, we got down to it. Ellie selected scripts for us, and we took turns in the recording booth. She chose a rather challenging John Cheever piece for me (which, she later told me, she reserved only for those she thought might have "something special"). I stood at the microphone, took a breath, and read the words, giving proper weight to certain phrases and employing beats and pauses for dramatic effect. I liked it. So did she.

At the end of our session, when the other two people had left, I lingered and talked with Ellie about the possibility of working one-on-one. She said yes, she was available. She also told me that she thought I had a natural talent for this work.

In our first private session, we talked a bit about my background and my as-yet unformed intentions. She presented me with a bit of narration to read. "Take all the time you need." I stood up at the microphone and read the copy, listening to my own voice as I spoke the words. When I finished, Ellie smiled and said, "You have a good voice, but don't fall in love with it. Voiceover acting is not about the voice, it's about the truth."

Over time, I came to understand what she meant. I noticed immediately, while recording (and certainly on playback), when I was *listening* to my voice. At those moments I lost all natural authenticity and began 'acting.' We also discovered that I had a 'default,' slipping into rather formal sonority, serious and sometimes rather professorial. It was pleasant to hear, but far from the truth we sought in performance.

I realized that if I was preoccupied with the words on the page or the impression I wanted to make, I could not speak the truth. The truth is elusive and requires surrender, so that it might arise from deep within—from the inside out, not the outside in. It disappears when forced. In a way, it's like meditation, in which it is best not to try to overcome anything, as that only adds fuel to the battle going on. Peace arises not from 'mind over matter,' but from the relaxation of both. If the mind races about, let it be. That is its nature. Attend to your breath. It will take you home.

A couple of years into our work, I chose a monologue from the film *The Lion in Winter*. In this scene, King Henry II, played by Peter O'Toole, confronts his three sons who have betrayed him. He brutally cuts them off from his life and bolts from the room, stumbling down the castle staircase, falling against the wall, and collapsing in despair at what he has done.

I affixed the script on to the television screen in my apartment and stood in front of it while Ellie sat nearby. I performed the words—again and again and again—each time doing my best to shed all preoccupations with the writing and my memory of O'Toole's incomparable performance. On the twelfth take, I was exhausted and wanted to stop, but looked over at Ellie and said, "One more time."

By then, I had memorized the monologue, and no longer needed to look at the script. The words and the meaning of the words now resided within. I was bone-weary and desolate, much like the king.

I did the read and something arose from deep down. As I raged and grieved, tears ran down my cheeks. When I finished, I looked over to Ellie. She was crying.

"What just happened?" I asked.

"Something extraordinary. Something sacred."

"I want to hold on to it. How do I hold on to it?"

"You don't need to hold on to it. It's yours now." It was a breakthrough experience, and taught me an enormous lesson: to allow the truth to arise, one must surrender all attempts to 'accomplish' or 'achieve' anything.

"I can't take credit for this at all. I didn't *do* anything. It did me."

"The work can't do you, until you put in the work."

Of course, she was right. Although acting, whether voiceover or on the stage or screen, is called *playing* a role, it requires an enormous amount of work. Only after putting in that work can one at last surrender. Then, perhaps, the truth will appear. And when the truth appears, Ellie said, "one can fulfill the paramount role of any actor:

service—to the writer, to their fellow actors, and to the audience, those fragile souls sitting in the dark."

And, I might add, to those children lying in their bedrooms, listening with their eyes closed.

Out of Print and Impossible to Find

Let me take you back in time: the year is 1984, before the Internet, before we could buy anything, anytime, from anywhere. On a hot, humid summer day in New York City, I was looking for a book.

But first: back in the early '70s, I had read a book titled *A Death in the Family* by the gifted and poetic American writer James Agee. It had won the Pulitzer Prize, and for good reasons. It is the deeply moving story of the impact on a family of the death of the father, much of it from the young son's point of view—and much of it from Agee's own experience of losing his father as a boy.

Sometime later I read *Let Us Now Praise Famous Men*, Agee's tribute to the desperately impoverished sharecropping families of the South during the Great Depression, illustrated with stark, haunting photographs by Walker Evans. I had never read anything so mysterious, so beautiful, before or since. I decided I wanted to read and have on my shelf everything Agee had written. And so began my quest.

In those days there were many small used-bookshops in New York, particularly in Greenwich Village and the Upper West Side. Whenever I was out for a walk in those neighborhoods, I stopped in and went right to the beginning of the shelves, where the *A*s were.

Over time, I was successful in finding everything Agee had written: novels, short stories, letters, poems, film critiques, screenplays—everything, that is, except one short novel, *The Morning Watch*, the story of a boy's quest for an epiphany on Easter Sunday. The book had been out of print for many years, and was simply impossible to find. And besides that, the used-bookshops were beginning to disappear.

*

It was a hot, humid summer day in New York City—the kind of day when boundaries blur and anything can happen. I left my apartment on Charles Street in the Village and headed north up West Fourth.

There he was. There he *always* was, the odd man with the dark, long hair, standing in front of his apartment building, leaning against the railing, wearing a raincoat no matter what the weather, or the season. I picked up my pace and walked past him—but not before hearing him mutter, "Books … books."

I stopped and turned around. "Do you sell books?"

Wordlessly, he turned and walked around the railing and down the steps. I hesitated, but my quest overcame whatever misgivings I had following a stranger into a dark basement apartment. Light filtered in through the dirty windows, and my eyes adjusted. There were *thousands* of books there, not arranged horizontally on shelves, but in vertical stacks, floor to ceiling. Dozens of pillars of books.

"I've been looking for a book by James Agee called *The Morning Watch*. It's been out of print for years. I wonder if you've ever heard of it."

Still without a word, he walked over to a ladder in the corner of the room and carried it to one of the stacks. He slowly climbed the steps, then reached up and plucked a small book from the very top.

He handed it down to me: *The Morning Watch* by James Agee. I stared at it, speechless. At last: "How much?"

"Two bucks."

I pulled out two singles from my wallet and handed them over.

"Wanna bag?"

"No thanks."

I turned and walked across the room, out the door and up the steps, back to the bright sidewalk—my book in my hand, and a story to tell.

Used

For those of us who suffer from Obsessive-Compulsive Disorder, a used book presents several challenges. First of all, it's *used.* Others have held it, written in it, soiled it with their fingers. Who would want such a book?

Back in the 1980s, I worked for an organization in New York City called the International Peace Academy. Located across the street from the United Nations, it was best known for offering training in peacekeeping and negotiation. We were highly regarded for our work and our discretion. Indeed, when, publicly, Israel and Palestine were not speaking, privately they *were*—in our offices.

When it came time for me to move on to other opportunities, the president of the organization, General Indar Jit Rikhye, who had been an adviser to UN Secretaries-General Dag Hammarskjöld and U Thant, presented me with a copy of the book we used in our training, which he inscribed meaningfully. I was very moved by his gesture of appreciation. When I got to my apartment, I opened the book and noticed handwriting in the margins; portions of the book had been underlined as well. He had given me a used book!

So that's what he thought of me. My reaction was so powerful and troubling that I brought the book along with me to my next therapy session. "Phyllis, General Rikhye gave me this book when I left the Academy. It's been used!"

"May I hold it?" I handed it to her and she leafed through it, smiling. "Yes, it's been used."

"That's what I said. He gave me a used book. What kind of a gift is that?"

"It's been used by someone learning how to make peace."

Now, in therapy that's called a "reframe": placing a troubling experience into a different context, which then changes the experience. Suddenly, the book took on far greater significance than a pristine volume with no history of use would have. It became meaningful. It became precious.

When I was in training at Bellevue, we had a shorthand way of describing people along the spectrum of emotional disorders: *too tightly wrapped* or *too loosely wrapped*. I resided at the former end of the continuum, but this experience with the book changed me. I now saw things that were used by others as invested with history and mystery, much as I had done when I was a child and would check out a well-worn book from the library and wonder who else had held it and read it.

That said, I will still go into a bookshop seeking a much-wanted volume, only to discover to my dismay that the single copy left on the shelf has a corner bent by another seeker: even before it's purchased, a book can be used. No sale. Such are the inconsistencies of insightful liberation from one's neuroses. Sometimes yes, sometimes no … sometimes sometimes.

As I have grown older, however, I have noticed my grip loosen on the quest for perfection. So have my friends. Some years ago, I had a reunion of old New York pals at my home in the desert: Patty, Sandy, Nan, Mike, Kate and Ron, Helen and Fred—all in our white terrycloth robes, out of which we were rarely seen.

We spent several wonderful days together, all talking at once, remembering and misremembering shared past experiences over decades of friendship. One day, Fred said to me, "You really seem a lot looser these days, a lot more comfortable." Such an observation, especially when given spontaneously, cannot help but be true.

On a subsequent visit, Fred, knowing of my admiration for his work with Jim Henson and the Muppets—for which he earned several Emmys—gave me one of those awards. "I want something of mine always to be out here in the desert," he said.

The gift was used. I keep it shined.

John Wanted You to Have This

Throughout my life, I have admired extraordinary people and have collected objects related to them, things they touched, things they owned. These tangible mementos are touchstones of memory, something to hold close. One of these people is Pope John XXIII.

In October 1958, the seventy-seven-year-old Italian Cardinal Angelo Giuseppe Roncalli was elected to the papal throne as a compromise between the liberal and conservative wings within the College of Cardinals, then in deep disagreement. It was thought that his reign would be relatively brief and unremarkable—a caretaker papacy. That was not to be the case. Upon donning the papal vestments, John experienced a certain stuffiness within the Church. He decided to open the windows and the doors. He met with leaders of other religions, including 130 members of a United Jewish Appeal delegation in 1960, greeting them with a verse from Genesis 45:4: "I am Joseph [i.e. Giuseppe], your brother."

In 1959, not long after he was elevated to the papacy, he made a significant change to the Good Friday service. Until that time, its Latin liturgy contained what many considered antisemitic language of contempt in its prayer for the conversion of the Jews: *Let us pray for the faithless [Latin:* perfidis*] Jews: that Almighty God may remove the veil from their hearts; so that they too may acknowledge Jesus Christ our Lord. Almighty and eternal God, who dost not exclude from thy mercy even Jewish faithlessness: hear our prayers, which we offer for the blindness of that people; that acknowledging the light of thy Truth, which is Christ, they may be delivered from their darkness. Through the same our Lord Jesus Christ, who liveth and reigneth with Thee in the unity of the Holy Spirit, God, for ever and ever. Amen.*

John had the offensive word *perfidis* removed. However, ritual habits are difficult to change. When a canon was celebrating the Good Friday service before the Pope in St Peter's Basilica in April 1963 and employed the old language, John stopped him in the middle of the service: "Begin again."

Pope John XXIII convened the Second Vatican Council in 1962, which, among other things, was meant to adapt Roman Catholicism to the modern world. Major changes in the Church were proposed. The Council took a close look at the liturgy. It was decided that people should hear the Mass in their own language, their own vernacular, rather than archaic Latin, and that the priest should face his congregation rather than have his back to them. Music and singing were granted a place. Women were subsequently invited to play roles as lectors, acolytes, and altar servers. The Church's orientation toward the Jewish people in particular underwent a radical change. Jews were now not to be considered as Other, but as brothers and sisters under the same God.

Not long before he died in June 1963, John composed a prayer to Christ in atonement for the Church's history of antisemitism: "We realize now that many, many centuries of blindness have dimmed our eyes, so that we no longer see the beauty of Thy Chosen People and no longer recognize in their faces the features of our first-born brother. We realize that our brows are branded with the mark of Cain. Centuries long has Abel lain in blood and tears, because we had forgotten Thy love. Forgive us the curse which we unjustly laid on the name of the Jews. Forgive us that, with our curse, we crucified Thee a second time."

As a Jew, I felt a deep appreciation for these extraordinary gestures from a man I had grown to admire and love—a man with whom, despite the differences in our beliefs, I felt a kinship.

Following a visit to St Peter's Basilica during the papal reign of John Paul II, I took the narrow stairway down to the shop. There were pictures, prayer cards, books, medals—all with the image of John Paul II. I approached one of the nuns who worked there.

"Hello, I'm looking for a medal that depicts Pope John XXIII. Might you have one?"

"Let's see," she said in a lilting Indian accent. She opened a large drawer filled with bronze medals. "John Paul … John Paul … John Paul … John Paul." She looked at every one of the dozens of medals. Finally, reaching into the shadows at the back of the drawer, she found a single medal with the image of John XXIII. She handed it to me, a gift: "John wanted you to have this."

The Brothers

My association with the Kennedy family began in 1960, when I was eleven years old. On my boyhood desk, I had before me a large, framed photograph of John F. Kennedy, my first hero, who watched over me as I toiled away at arithmetic problems. It was the spring of 1960, and every afternoon after homework I hopped on my bike and rode to the corner of Main Street and New York Avenue, where I enthusiastically handed out JFK campaign bumper stickers. Then my man won the presidency—undoubtedly, I thought, in part due to my earnest efforts.

The year 1960 was an exciting time for a boy who was just beginning to peek out beyond the perimeter of family and community to the wider world. There was this young man who spoke of the great promise and responsibility of the next generation of Americans. That next generation included me, and I felt, perhaps for the first time, part of something much larger than myself. For my volunteer efforts, I was awarded a little silver *PT 109* campaign pin—the emblem of JFK's heroism in World War II, a precious souvenir that I still wear on my lapel.

When John Kennedy became President, it was as if the world, which we had been observing in shades of black and white, suddenly turned to full color. I watched him on TV. I listened to his speeches. I read his books. I pinned my hopes on him.

The New Frontier, a vision of a young, vital, and generous America, captivated my imagination. It all began with his inaugural address—at once a proclamation of freedom, a declaration of strength, and an appeal for peace. In the thousand days that followed, I watched extraordinary things unfold: the Food for Peace program, the Alliance for Progress, the Peace Corps, civil rights legislation, arts initiatives, the space program, the Nuclear Test Ban Treaty. Along with the rest of the world, I held my breath during the Cuban Missile Crisis, all the way to its successful and peaceful resolution.

During a time when our country was altogether mesmerized by the communist threat, I heard our president frankly acknowledge our differences with the Soviet Union, but then say:

> … in the final analysis, our most basic common link is that we all inhabit this small planet. We all breathe the same air. We all cherish our children's future. And we are all mortal.

In those few unprecedented words, he transcended the constricted boundaries of our thinking and pointed us toward a new vision of our country and the world, a world of common purpose, a world at peace.

Years later, his daughter Caroline sent me a copy of a doodle her father had drawn. It was of the Presidential Seal. Instead of arrows in one talon and an olive branch in the other, the eagle held olive branches in both.

And then, he was gone.

*

Five years after the assassination of John F. Kennedy, in 1968, I worked on the staff of Robert F. Kennedy's presidential campaign in Maryland while attending college at Johns Hopkins. RFK's campaign was young, and it was difficult to even get campaign materials, so in some cases we made our own buttons and bumper stickers and flyers. We were a devoted bunch, and determined to get our man elected.

This was a different time, with different challenges. I, too, was different: older now, and far more aware of the injustices prevalent in our own country and in our relations with other nations. Robert Kennedy spoke to these issues with passion and clarity. He directed our gaze away from ourselves, and toward those whom we had forgotten in our midst. He called upon us to hear the voices of those who suffer from afar. And by informing our political discourse with both compassion and commitment to action, he demonstrated the possibility of elevating our lives through service.

He had been transformed by his brother's death. He carried his inconsolable grief in his eyes. It was present in his posture. When he visited Bedford-Stuyvesant and Watts and Appalachia and the Mississippi Delta and the migrant farmers' fields, and said that it was "unacceptable" that people in our country should live this way, the people he met, the people whose lives were bent by pain and sorrow, saw something in this slight young man that they recognized. They saw his suffering, and they trusted him with theirs. He became their voice, and carried their hope.

Robert Kennedy spoke with equal fervor about the necessity of ending the war in Vietnam, a war that was not only unspeakable in its brutality, but also was being executed in violation of everything decent for which this country stands.

When he spoke of these and other problems, he called upon the young to accept their responsibility to lead us toward a just and humane future. Before a group of students in South Africa, he said:

> Few men are willing to brave the disapproval of their fellows, the censure of their colleagues, the wrath of their society. Moral courage is a rarer commodity than bravery in battle or great intelligence. Yet it is the one essential, vital quality for those who seek to change the world which yields most painfully to change … I believe that in this generation those with the courage to enter the conflict will find themselves with companions in every corner of the world.

And then, he was gone.

*

When I returned to university in the fall of 1968, I wanted to do something to honor John and Robert Kennedy, and so I created the Kennedy Lectureship on International Affairs, which was to take place on campus every spring. I wrote to Senator Edward Kennedy, inviting him to give the first address of the lectureship. He wrote back that he would have liked to, but that he could not, because of other commitments at the time. With a boldness that astonishes me now, I replied that I would delay the inaugural lectureship until he was available. And so, a year passed.

During that time, I hand-delivered more letters to the senator's office, and got to know several members of his staff—including Melody Miller, at the time his receptionist and later to become Senior Aide and spokesperson for the Kennedy family. They became my allies in encouraging Senator Kennedy to accept my invitation.

In February 1970, the senator wrote to me with six proposed dates and said, "you choose." I selected the evening of Wednesday 6 May. Preparations were made. In case we had overflow from the auditorium, I arranged for loudspeakers outside Shriver Hall, so that those standing on the grass in the quadrangle could hear the senator's speech. The day approached.

On Monday 4 May, National Guardsmen shot and killed four unarmed students and wounded nine at Kent State University, during a non-violent student protest of President Richard Nixon's expansion of the Vietnam War into Cambodia. The country reeled; already torn apart by the war, it was now further fractured by this act of violence on our own soil against our young. We urgently searched the horizon for someone to lead us out of the darkness.

Two nights later, I met Senator Kennedy's car at the foot of the marble steps of Shriver Hall. As we ascended, I placed my hand at his back, touching a legacy of both pain and hope.

About 1,200 people filled the auditorium that night, and another 4,000 stood outside in the quadrangle, holding candles under the stars, listening to Edward Kennedy's impassioned plea for peace.

A month or so after the speech, I brought a portfolio of photographs to the senator. I sat in his outer office with three other people waiting to see him. Suddenly he rushed in, took a look at us and said, "Dean, come on in."

We sat together on a small couch as he slowly turned the pages—as if he had nothing else to do—and reflected on his experience at the lectureship. I handed him a photo and asked if he might sign it for me. He took it to his desk, where he sat for a long time, head in hand. As I looked at him, it crossed my mind that this was the loneliest man I had ever seen. He brought the photograph back to me. He had written:

> To Dean Rudoy—With warm memories of my visit to Johns Hopkins and with the hope that you continue your concern and interest in the problems of our country.—*Ted Kennedy*

A couple of years later, I wrote a little book called *Armed and Alone: The American Security Dilemma*, and asked Senator Kennedy if he would write the introduction. He kindly agreed. We remained in touch. I also remained in touch with Melody, who became a very dear friend. One evening, when I was in Washington, after everyone else had gone home, we sat out on the senator's office balcony overlooking the Capitol Building, drinking sodas and believing that, if we reached out far enough, we could touch the dome so brightly lit for all to see. We spoke of him.

As his brothers were before him, Senator Kennedy was committed to extending the perimeter of freedom, equality, economic opportunity, and social justice to all Americans. Having not received the presidential nomination of his party, he closed his conciliation speech at the 1980 Democratic National Convention with:

> It is the glory and the greatness of our tradition to speak for those who have no voice, to remember those who are forgotten … For all those whose cares have been our concern, the work goes on, the cause endures, the hope still lives, and the dream shall never die.

And then, he was gone.

*

These three men had a remarkable impact on the development of my character. John Kennedy helped to shape my mind; Robert Kennedy helped to shape my heart; Edward Kennedy helped to shape my conscience.

Each manifested in his life a coincidence of opposites: they were at once idealists and realists, romantic and pragmatic. Earnest and audacious, they elevated the political discourse in this country and outlined a trajectory of high purpose for America—a generous America that would deliver on its promise. They had a vision in which people were free and nations were just; in which the fundamental principles of liberty, equality, and human dignity would guide the conduct of a world at peace.

The Kennedy brothers mean something to me because of who I am, and who I am has something to do with the Kennedy brothers. My gratitude for them has only increased with the passage of time.

*

Thirty years after I created The Kennedy Lectureship at Johns Hopkins, it was my honor to sponsor the Robert F. Kennedy Conference at the John F. Kennedy Presidential Library on 25 November 2000, in celebration of the seventy-fifth anniversary of RFK's birth.

Not long after that, I became involved with the Robert F. Kennedy Center for Justice and Human Rights, sponsoring its annual Human Rights Award for ten years, serving on its Board of Directors, and now serving as Trustee. It pleases me to think that, in some small way, I have contributed to the extension of the legacy of these men into the future, where it belongs.

Following my retirement from the RFK Center Board of Directors, at our annual Human Rights Award luncheon in Washington, there was a clinking of a glass. The Chairman of the Board rose from his seat: "I rise to recognize a man whose dedication to the legacy of Robert Kennedy is unparalleled." We all looked around the room. "Dean, would you please come up here?"

I stood and walked to the head table. Ethel Kennedy reached behind her and lifted up a bust of her husband, which she presented to me. Inscribed on its base were these words: FOR DEAN—WHO ALSO MAKES GENTLE THE LIFE OF THE WORLD. LOVE, ETHEL. I knew the reference. On the night of 4 April 1968, in an unplanned outdoor speech in Indianapolis, Robert Kennedy delivered to his listeners the news of the death of Martin Luther King, Jr. He closed his remarks with these words:

> Let us dedicate ourselves to what the Greeks wrote so many years ago: to tame the savageness of man and make gentle the life of this world. Let us dedicate ourselves to that, and say a prayer for our country and for our people.

The journey was complete: from a street corner in Oshkosh, Wisconsin, to a head table in Washington, DC. And in my hands, the most precious of possessions, a tangible reminder of a good and decent man.

Losing My Grip

Having acquired and accumulated a lot of *stuff* over seven decades, I wonder, why this habit of possession? I've also been thinking of my death recently—not my *death*, actually, but my absence ... the absence of my presence. When I have slipped out of form and disappeared from view, what will be left behind? What will have meaning?

It's pretty obvious, although we all often forget it, that whatever we *get* in this life disappears along with us. It is only what we *give* that outlasts us. There is an old Yiddish expression: "A shroud has no pockets." It's a gentle reminder of the vanity of our attempts to hold on, the futility of attachment to things. But it's not just a comment about death; it's an encouragement to give in life, rather than receive or take.

Having recently recovered from a serious illness, I recall that in the midst of it, I became obsessed with the pile of stuff I was leaving behind for someone else to sort through. To save them the trouble, I began to engage in a project of jettisoning unnecessary ballast. *Ballast*—maybe that has something to do with why I have amassed so much: to have enough in my hold so as not to capsize. Well, looking around at the piles of things on counters, in cabinets, and tucked away in drawers, I don't think I am in any danger of tipping over. In fact, I believe much of this stuff is holding me down and in place, and keeping me from sailing to new harbors of expression and discovery. Flotsam and jetsam are not ballast; they are baggage.

Maybe it has something to do with identity. Are my possessions extensions of myself? Perhaps. Pretty much everything I own reflects my interests and passions, and looking at my stuff is sort of like seeing a version of myself. However, every morning, when I do my exercises outside, looking out at the desert landscape, the big sky, and the long horizon, feeling rather light and free and grateful, I think: *Do I really need any of that stuff back there in the house? If it were all to vanish, would I disappear?*

While considering the pain of life and the mystery of death, Hamlet declares: "To be, or not to be, that is the question." With a respectful bow to Mr Shakespeare, I propose: "To be *and* not to be, that is the answer."

If we think about it, every breath we take represents this paradox: we breathe in (to be) … we breathe out (not to be). There is something to be said for that natural, uninterrupted rhythm. If we hold our breath, we lose it. If we let it go, it returns to us. The ocean waves come in to the shore (to be) and then return to the sea (not to be). The waves are just a momentary manifestation of the ocean waving. Buddhists tell us that everything in this life is in the process of arising, manifesting, and dissolving. Everything comes into form, then goes out of form. All forms are temporary, including us.

That recognition might make some of us sad. But, it shouldn't. It just is what it is, and what it is for we human beings is a balancing act between attachment and surrender.

I am now in my eighth decade. It happened so quickly, after taking so long. But time marches on, and I have a few observations.

I am now over the hill. On my way to its apex, having pretty much always been attracted by the next shiny object, you can imagine my delight at seeing something at the top that glistened in the sunlight. I assumed it was a prize to acquire. Upon arriving, however, I discovered it was something far more valuable: a mirror. And in that mirror I saw my reflection: an old and mortal man. I was reminded of the Zen lesson that one's mind should be like a mirror, which *accepts* everything, *rejects* nothing, *receives*, but does not *keep*.

Some years ago, the University of New Mexico invited porcelain artist and Japanese National Living Treasure Inoue Manji Sensei to teach a ceramics class. He assigned every student the same task: to make the finest tea bowl they could. As the semester went by, and the students labored with clay and glaze, many of their first bowls were discarded, or broke under fire in the kiln. At the end of the course, the master had them stand in a circle, holding their finest work in their cupped hands. Then came his final instruction: "Let them go." And they all shattered to the ground.

Buddhists suggest that all suffering emanates from attachment—our human nature to grasp, to accumulate, to own—whether those things are material, intellectual, or spiritual. Possessing things gives the ego the illusion of permanence in a world of constant change and uncertainty. It's understandable. Who wouldn't want a safe harbor when the seas become stormy? But the truth is, nothing lasts forever; to try to hold on to anything or anyone leads only to a fear of its loss. The Buddha is often depicted sitting with his hands open and empty, palms up, with that slight smile on his serene face.

While looking at myself in that mirror at the top of the hill, something started to give way. My stance in life began to shift: from assets to awareness, from acquisitions to awe. A metamorphosis began to take place. I found myself grasping a bit less, giving a bit more.

It seems that there are two "A" lists by which I was to guide my conduct on each side of the hill. The first can be seen as composed of rather masculine traits; the second, feminine. While I climbed up the first side of the hill, I was naturally occupied with things I could *grasp for myself*—asserting, achieving, accomplishing, acquiring, and accumulating.

I was lucky to reach the apex. What now? I have become aware of my mortality, and have come to a different understanding of what gives meaning to life, and why I am here. My hands have begun to open. I have begun, only just begun, to let go of things—not just objects, but also attitudes, such as jealousy and judgment.

While I have been making my way carefully down the other side of the hill, I have become occupied with things only I can *give to others*: my attention, affection, admiration, appreciation, and—perhaps the finest human gift, whether offered or received—acceptance.

But what if I am called upon to give something I do not have? The miracle of the human spirit is this: we can give what we do not have, even what we never received, even what was taken from us. This is true for each of the gifts above.

In need of attention? *Give attention.* In need of affection, admiration, appreciation, acceptance? *Give them.*

In so doing, I have discovered that my needs have been met. Much as when one candle lights another and is not diminished in giving its gift, but *enhanced* in giving, I have received. And in this life, only that which is given is not lost.

A simple story: I visited some friends and their little son Sam, about a year old. During an animated conversation I was having with him, Sam lifted a Cheerio—a happy little morsel of nutrition—from those scattered in front of him, and reached toward my mouth. I opened, and in it went. Sam was delighted. So much for the Cheerio.

A Jewish folktale holds that when we die, we all go to the same place, and we are exactly as we are, except we can't bend our elbows. The wicked suffer because they cannot feed themselves. The virtuous learn to feed each other.

Two stories that point to the same truth: *we are meant to take care of one another.*

It would be good to awaken fully to these lessons before I go to sleep. And when it comes time to lie down at last and wrap the drapery of my couch about me, wouldn't it be fine to let my last breath put wind into someone else's sails? Just around the corner, there will be someone whose need my heart knows well, and knowing well, can fulfill.

Ram Dass says: *we're all just walking each other home.* It would be best, then, to open my grip and let things go, so that I am free to hold another's hand.

Epilogue: Return to Eden

It is written that two trees stood at opposite ends in the Garden of Eden from which God instructed Adam and Eve they must not eat. One was called the Tree of Knowledge of Good and Evil; the other, the Tree of Everlasting Life.

Though what transpired there one afternoon occurred quite some time ago, the story is well-known. God—Who, it is said, knows everything—was getting a bit bored with perfection, so He placed within Adam and Eve *yetzer hara* (an inclination to do evil) and *yetzer hatov* (an inclination to do good). By nature, amongst these and other personality features, Adam and Eve were curious. This characteristic had a role in what followed. Serpent invited Eve to eat an apple from the Tree of Knowledge of Good and Evil, in order to know what God knew. It tasted good. She offered some to Adam. Pretty much always hungry, he took a bite. The story goes on from there, but, bottom line, the couple was expelled from Eden for disobedience. We've been sitting in detention ever since.

Now, it is important to remember that the apple came from the Tree of *Knowledge* of Good and Evil. Having eaten the fruit, Adam and Eve no longer experienced the Oneness from which they came, and to which they immediately yearned to return. They were cast out—off the Earth and into a world of opposites, dualities, polarities, and dichotomies. No longer in the eternal present, they now had a past and a future. Immediately upon being thrust from Eden, the young couple began a journey to find their way back, over the river and through the woods.

Adam and Eve—and all their descendants throughout the millennia—have, for some time, been on an heroic journey. As with all such journeys, there are three parts to the adventure: separation, initiation, and return. The separation occurred in Eden—in the past, *there and then*. The initiation is occurring in our time—in the present, *here and now*. The return is up ahead—in the future, *if and when*.

As with all initiations, one must go through an ordeal that tries one's soul and tempers one's spirit, leading to a transformation of one's self. This book is about such an initiation. It is also about our return to Eden. For, though banished from the Oneness, our expulsion was never meant to be permanent.

There is, after all, another tree.

*

On second thought, is it possible that, at that fated moment in time, it was only our *perception* that changed, not our location? Is it possible that we never left?

There is abundant evidence all around us. The stories in this book can be seen as glimpses of Eden in which emissaries appear, disguised in different forms—human, animal, and natural—all carrying dispatches from a place of Oneness, all advocates of our well-being.

It is in the evening of my life, that fugitive space of time in which everything evens out, boundaries blur, opposites combine, that I have come to understand these things. Nonetheless, I am mindful of the cautionary adage: *We do not see things as they are; we see things as we are.* Although I may point at something I see, you might perceive something quite different. That's just fine, as long as your eyes are open.

We all stand upon the Earth, so it shouldn't be too hard to find common ground. Perhaps, as you have read this book, there have been moments when you have been moved or delighted, moments of recognition. If that is the case, in those moments, we have both returned to Eden.

Welcome home.

About the Author

After graduating college in 1971 from The Johns Hopkins University, Dean William Rudoy was off to Washington, DC to stop the war, working with various peace groups and United States Senators. He published two books: *Violence: The Crisis of American Confidence* (1971) and *Armed and Alone: The American Security Dilemma* (1972).

In New York City, following his training at the New York University-Bellevue Medical Center, he received his doctorate in clinical psychology from Fordham University in 1985. He then practiced, with a focus on children and adolescents. In 1989, he left the gruff embrace of Manhattan for the tender hold of the New Mexico desert to teach, practice, speak, and write.

All along the way, he has been devoted to causes: children, peace, social justice, human rights. He has been a consultant to national and international organizations, and has sat on various non-profit boards. He currently serves on the Board of Trustees of The Robert F. Kennedy Center for Justice and Human Rights.

www.deanrudoy.com